Polly swept her gaze up to take in the full view of the stranger standing in her driveway.

She saw the cowboy boots first. They totally set the tone for what was to come—jeans, denim shirt over broad shoulders. From what she could see in the shadow of the brim of his dark brown cowboy hat, he had a likeable face, not too handsome, not too rugged, and a subtle but earnest smile.

"I was passing by on my way home, saw you lying in your driveway under your car and I thought, well, either *A*, you had run over yourself, in which case you'd have a story I couldn't miss hearing." His smile took on a hint of teasing. "Or *B*, I thought maybe you could use a hand."

"*B*, definitely *B*." Polly smiled.

"Sam Goodacre." He took her hand in his.

Their eyes met and held. She had been in town for all of a few hours and already met a guy who made her heart race. So much for taking things at a slower pace here….

Books by Annie Jones

Love Inspired

April in Bloom
Somebody's Baby
Somebody's Santa
Somebody's Hero
Marrying Minister Right
Blessings of the Season
  "The Holiday Husband"
Their First Noel
Home to Stay
Triplets Find a Mom

Love Inspired Single Title

Sadie-in-Waiting
Mom Over Miami
The Sisterhood of the
  Queen Mamas

ANNIE JONES

Winner of a Holt Medallion for Southern-themed fiction, and the *Houston Chronicle*'s Best Christian Fiction Author of 1999, Annie Jones grew up in a family that loved to laugh, eat and talk—often all at the same time. They instilled in her the gift of sharing through words and humor, and the confidence to go after her heart's desire (and to act fast if she wanted the last chicken leg). A former social worker, she feels called to be a "voice for the voiceless" and has carried that calling into her writing by creating characters often overlooked in our fast-paced culture—from seventysomethings who still have a zest for life to women over thirty with big mouths and hearts to match. Having moved thirteen times during her marriage, she is currently living in rural Kentucky with her husband and two children.

Triplets Find a Mom
Annie Jones

Love Inspired

Recycling programs
for this product may
not exist in your area.

LOVE INSPIRED BOOKS

ISBN-13: 978-0-373-87729-4

TRIPLETS FIND A MOM

www.LoveInspiredBooks.com

Printed in U.S.A.

If your gift is serving others, serve them well.
If you are a teacher, teach well.
—*Romans* 12:7

For Emma Dobben and Alleyah Asher
and whoever comes along after—
I am looking at YOU Rob and Melissa—to share
our love and grow our family in God's promises!

Chapter One

If you can't beat 'em...run away.

The finality of the moving truck trundling off made the last thing her sister had said to her loom large in Polly Bennett's thoughts. Too exhausted to move, she stood hip-deep in the stacks of boxes in her rented two-bedroom cottage five hundred miles from everyone she knew. She eased out a long, satisfied breath and smiled. For once in their twenty-six years on this earth, Esther, Polly's identical twin sister, was wrong. Polly hadn't run away from anything; she had run *to* something.

Polly had run *to* the place where she would build a life, pursue a career, make a difference in people's lives. She closed her eyes to form a short, silent prayer that this would be the place where she would meet a great guy, fall in love and raise a family—where she would make her home.

"Amen," Polly whispered, her heart light and her head swirling with a million things she needed to get done. She moved around the boxes that held the contents of her life, boxes marked Kitchen and Living

Room and Fragile. She took a deep breath, tugged open the uppermost one and immediately recognized a series of paper-wrapped rectangles. The newsprint packaging rattled as she uncovered a set of four sleek silver frames. Her shoes squeaked on the polished wood floor as she went to put the series of family photos on the mantel of the painted brick fireplace.

"Giving y'all the best spot in the house to watch over me…" she murmured in her soft Georgia accent. First she placed the photo of her brother and sister-in-law and their two kids, who looked as if they'd stepped out of a catalog of perfect families, then added, "But not be able to tell me I'm doing it all wrong."

Next she settled in the photos of her mom and her mom's new husband, and her dad and her dad's soon-to-be next wife, on either side of the first frame. The second she did it, she felt a cloud of heaviness in her chest, so she moved them both onto the same side. That did little to ease the ache in her heart over her parents' split, even though it had happened almost sixteen years ago. Finally she arranged the pictures so that if you stood in just the right spot and gazed at them at just the right angle, you would see the two faces of the parents she loved so dearly side by side. That helped.

A little.

One last frame to unwrap. Polly tugged it free and let the paper tumble down over her ratty tennis shoes. Her eyes lingered over the image of herself and her sister seated on either side of a wrought-iron table under a red-and-white-striped restaurant awning. Unlike the others, it was not a professional portrait but a shot taken the day her sister had accepted her job as first assistant chef. That same day Polly had decided to quit working as a permanent substitute teacher and find her way in the world, wherever that quest took her.

Esther's hair was pulled back so tight that if it were blond instead of jet-black, she might have looked bald. Polly had to peer closely to see the slip of a ponytail high on the back of Esther's head. In contrast, Polly's unruly black hair, which was only a little bit shorter than Essie's, fell forward over one dark eyebrow. It flipped up at the ends against her shirt collar and stuck out on one side.

While Essie's makeup was simple and perfect, Polly had chosen that day to try something dramatic with eyeliner, making her dark pupils look almost black. And despite the fact that Essie worked preparing food in a hot and hectic restaurant kitchen all day long, she looked crisp and cool. Polly was the one with an orangey cheese snack smudge on her shoulder, from where one of her students had hugged her.

She shook her head and sang under her breath, "'One of these things is not like the other...'"

Deeper in the box, she found the big envelope containing her letter of acceptance as the newest second-grade teacher at Van Buren Elementary School. She took it out and hugged it to her chest, filled with gratitude for the last-minute decision by an older teacher to retire that had resulted in Polly getting the chance of a lifetime.

Outside, the rustling of bushes, the snap of a twig made her pulse kick up. She checked out the curtain-less window in the front room. The long shadows of late afternoon made it impossible to see much, but the neatly kept houses settled cozily on the treelined street left her with a sense of well-being she had never really known. Renting it sight unseen after her video interview had worked out, after all. She couldn't help but smile at the sight. Even though she hadn't been in this town since she was six years old, she had known this was where she belonged.

"Baconburg, Ohio." She held out the envelope and trailed her fingers over the town's name on the return address then over the cancellation stamp dated July 15, just a little over two weeks ago. To the average person the letter was simply the confirmation of her last-minute contract offer. But to Polly? A flutter of excitement rose from the pit of her stomach and she gave a nervous laugh. "This is my ticket home."

Her whole life since that childhood move she'd felt as if she was at odds with...well, everything. She'd never found peace in Atlanta, Georgia, where her parents had moved to make a better life for their family.

Polly shook her head and sighed, but that did not even begin to unravel the knot in her chest that the memories of those early years in Atlanta always brought. *Better?*

Richer. Faster. More driven, maybe. But better?

Polly didn't see it. The fighting between her parents had started not long after that move and escalated with the driving pace of their lives in the city. They tried to hold the family together, and Polly tried to accept things how she'd been raised—that everything presented an opportunity to be seized, a competition to be won.

But the truth was that Polly just loved kids. Teaching them, guiding them, watching them grow and learn and embrace life in their own unique ways seemed like the greatest ambition anyone could have. Her family did not get that. Sometimes Polly felt her own family did not get her.

They especially did not get her longing to return to Baconburg.

"But here I am—" she swept her gaze over the unpacked boxes in her small house "—on my own. Alone."

The rustling under her front window interrupted her musings again. She set the envelope aside, went to the shallow window seat and peered out. Nothing. She sank to sit on the window seat. The rays of the late-afternoon sun slanted across the gleaming hardwood floor. So she was done running. Now what?

Her stomach grumbled and that seemed like the answer—eat something. She started to head toward the kitchen, then realized she didn't even have any food in the house.

If she were back in Atlanta she'd just hop in her little hybrid and scoot over to her sister's restaurant or over to her mom's house to raid the fridge. She certainly didn't know anyone well enough to do that here. She didn't really *know* anyone here. And the only restaurant she knew of in Baconburg was a fast-food spot out on the highway.

This time the noise outside sounded like a low whine. Probably a corner of one of the shaggy bushes scraping against the glass or the metal gutters creaking. A car pulled up in the drive across the street and two children came scrambling down the walk to greet the man climbing out from behind the wheel. Her stomach rumbled. The people went inside. She glanced over her shoulder at her family's photos on the mantel and it all hit her.

She had no one here. A wave of loneliness swept over her. Real loneliness. She always carried her faith within her and with it her connection to God and to all her friends and family, who routinely held one another in prayer. So it wasn't a matter of being completely abandoned. But…

Finally a clear whimper at her front door made her catch her breath. She shut her eyes, hoping again that she had only imagined it.

Another whimper.

Tension wound from between her shoulder blades through her body to tighten into a knot in the pit of her stomach.

She had seen that little dog hanging around her yard as she moved boxes in. She assumed it belonged to one of the families on the block and forced herself not to try to gather up the sweet-faced little animal.

You never get a second chance to make a first impression. Polly could practically hear her mother schooling her in an attempt to get the imperfect twin to be more like her sister. It must have sunk in a little because Polly had not wanted the first impression she made to be that she had stolen her neighbor's pet.

This time a series of three short whimpers, then a snuffle moved her to action. She went to the front door and opened it slowly. She'd just steal a peek and—

A soft golden-brown muzzle poked into the crack between the door and doorframe.

"Oh! No, puppy." She reached down to push the animal back outside. "This is not your home. You should go back where you belong."

A small, cold nose filled her palm followed by a soft warm tongue. She glanced down and her gaze met a pair of huge, soft brown eyes.

Polly was lost. She had always been a pushover for brown eyes. And these? Looking up at her from the sweetest little face of a doggy who, like her, wasn't sure if he would be welcome in this new environment. Oh, yeah, she was lost for sure.

"Okay, I'll take you in for the night, but starting tomorrow morning I am going to do everything I can to find your real own—" She'd hardly started to pull open the door when the animal nudged his way inside.

He had the elongated body and uncapped energy of a dachshund. The long ears and short, stocky legs of a basset hound maybe, but with the coloring, brown eyes and nose of a golden retriever. Tongue lapping and tail wagging, he jumped on her and threw her off-balance. She sank to the floor and the little guy squirmed into her lap, laid his head against her cheek and sighed.

For one fleeting moment her loneliness eased—until she realized she couldn't allow herself to get too attached. Her first responsibility to this little fellow was to get him back to those who loved him. Much like her duty as the town's new second-grade teacher was to encourage children to learn and grow and then to move on.

"Okay, let's get some food." She stood and brushed the dog hair off her clothes, snapped up her purse, then went to the door. "Tomorrow I'll run up to the school and get whatever I need to make some flyers."

She'd brought paper, markers, glue, scissors and other supplies with her from Atlanta because she didn't know what she'd find in Baconburg. "Then I can take a picture of you, scan it into my laptop, make a flyer and post them around town. But for *now?*" She opened the front door and motioned for him to follow. "Wanna go for a ride in the car?"

Apparently he did not.

"Come out from under there!" Gingerly, she poked her nose under the back end of her car where the dog had darted after she had stepped outside.

The puppy whimpered.

She recognized the sound of a car engine cutting off, a door opening and falling shut again. She couldn't stop to think about what kind of first impression she was making on some neighbor. Despite her thoughts on wanting to leave her competitive upbringing behind, she couldn't help herself—she was determined to win this little battle of wills. A battle not for her own benefit, but this time to help the frightened animal.

"Just a little closer…" Her cheek flattened against the cold bumper. She stretched out her hand, straining her fingers to try to reach some part of the animal. "I wish I could make you understand that this is for your own good. Can't you just give a little bit, too?"

"I know people who name their cars. Even some who give them pep talks or good swearing outs, but trying to guilt your car into running? That's totally new to me."

Polly gasped at the deep, masculine voice. She

wasn't frightened so much as mortified to be caught in this awkward position.

"Uh, hello, I wasn't… That is… Hang on a sec…" She knew it would take her a minute to work her arm back enough to get leverage so she could free herself. Maybe she should say something about how silly she looked to make him chuckle, but nothing sprang to mind.

"I, um, I was just… I wasn't talking to…" Heart racing, she finally got herself out from under the car, banging the back of her head on the plastic bumper as she did. That slight injury—more to her ego than her noggin—did not explain her reaction when she swept her gaze up to take in the full view of the stranger standing in her driveway.

She saw the cowboy boots first. They totally set the tone for what was to come—jeans, denim shirt over broad shoulders, a relaxed, open stance that instantly put her at ease. From what she could see in the shadow of the brim of his dark brown cowboy hat, he had a likable face, not too handsome, not too rugged, and a subtle but earnest smile.

"I was passing by on my way home. Saw you lying in your driveway under your car and I thought, well, either A, you had run over yourself, in which case you'd have a story I couldn't miss hearing." He used his left hand to tip his hat back. No wedding ring. His smile took on a hint of teasing. "Or B, I thought maybe you could use a hand."

He would have laughed if she'd said something about her silly situation while backing out and she sort of wished she'd done it now. There could be worse things than planting herself in this guy's memory. She swept back the fringe of her shaggy bangs, and stole a peek at the man's hunter-green truck parked at the end of her driveway with the painted logo Goodacre Organic Farm. The Farmer Sows the Word. Mark 4:14.

"B, definitely B." Polly smiled. A farmer and a Christian—who better to deal with one of God's creatures? "I could use some help, thank you."

"I'd be happy to take a look." He squatted down, sweeping his hat off as he did. Suddenly they were at eye level. And what warm brown eyes they were.

"I have to admit I don't know a lot about fixing cars, but I'm willing to give it a go." He settled the hat on the drive, then ran his hand back through the short-ish waves of sandy-brown hair. "What's the problem? Loose muffler? Oil leak?"

He bent down low to peer under the car. A cold nose thrust forward, a flash of tongue.

"Scared dog," Polly said, her timing just a bit off.

"Hey!" The man whipped his large hand across his chin and nailed Polly with a stunned look. "There's a dog under there."

"I know. *That's* who I was talking to." Hadn't she made that clear? The second she'd laid eyes on her champion farmer she'd had a hard time following the conversation. "Can you help me coax him out?"

"Does he bite?"

"He hasn't bitten me." She pressed her lips together to launch into a more thorough explanation, but he didn't give her time.

"All right, I'll give it a try." He clapped his hands together.

A soft woof came from beneath the car.

Polly sucked air between her teeth. "Thanks, I really appreciate your coming to our rescue. I guess this is one of the benefits of small-town living."

He opened his mouth to say something, but instead a woman's voice called out, "Hey, Sam! Need any help?"

"Got it under control, thanks!" The man, whose name was Sam, it seemed, waved back. He gave Polly a wry look, clearly not quite put out, not quite thrilled with the attention they had drawn. "Another 'benefit' of small-town life—wherever you go…there you are."

Polly gave a light laugh at the oversimplification of his frustration with being spotted.

"More precisely, there your friends are, or your family, or your pastor." He gave a shrug, then nodded to the car tag sporting a frame from an Atlanta auto dealer on the back of her little red car. "Not the kind of thing you have to worry about where you're from, I guess."

"Or here, actually. I'm Polly Bennett, by the way." She held out her hand.

"Sam Goodacre." He took her hand in his.

Their eyes met and held. She had been in town for all of a few hours and already met a guy who made her heart race. So much for taking things at a slower pace here. She drew in a deep breath of fresh summer air. "It's good to meet you. I just—"

A pathetic whimper from under the car kept her from launching into her story.

"Why don't you go around to the other side of the

car in case he heads that direction?" Sam directed her by drawing a circle with one finger.

Polly nodded and hurried around to the other side of the car and started to get down on one knee, but before she could, Sam's head popped up over the roof of her small vehicle.

"Got him." He lifted the dog up. Floppy ears and tongue flapped out, all landing in Sam's smiling face. "Yeah, yeah. No need to get all mushy about it... What's his name?"

She gave a big sigh at the overload of adorableness, then shifted her gaze to the pup. "I don't know."

"What?"

"He's a stray," she admitted, twisting her hands together. "I just saw him around earlier today. Then when I opened the door to check on him, he ran inside, then back outside and now I can't... I just... I couldn't..."

"Don't tell me. You've fallen in love with him already."

"Don't you believe in love at first sight?" Okay, that was way too flirty to say to a man she'd just met. Still, Polly tipped her head to one side and waited for his answer.

"Believe in it?" He lowered the dog out of face-licking range and gave a resigned kind of smile, his brown eyes framed by the faint beginnings of laugh lines. "I think it's unavoidable."

Her pulse went from racing to practically ricocheting through her body.

"Especially when you're talking about a little lost dog as cute as this." He looked down and rubbed the dog behind the ears, then came around the front end of the car to bring the animal to her.

"Of course." Polly let out a breath she hadn't even realized she'd been holding. "I still want to try to find who he belongs to, of course, but if nobody claims him…"

"He's a lucky dog." He bundled the dog into her waiting arms.

"I don't believe in luck." She ran her fingers along the dog's smooth, silky ear. "I believe in God's blessings."

"I've had a few of those in my life." He nodded but didn't offer any further explanation, just turned and headed for his truck.

"So…" Polly looked up and down the street, not sure what to do next. Her gaze fell on the truck. "Oh! Do you know… I mean, it's about food."

"I have been known to eat food, yes." He patted his flat stomach even as he slowed his pace slightly and spoke to her over his shoulder. "What do you want to know?"

I want to know that everything is going to work out fine. I want to know if I made the right choice moving here. I want to know when I'll see you *again.* "I don't have any dog food in the house, so I was going to take him with me to grab a fast-food burger. Do you think it would be okay if he ate one of those?"

"I think it would be okay if *you* ate one of them." He shook his head and scratched his fingers through his thick, light brown hair. "But there's a gas station with a little fresh market near the burger place. You can get a can of dog food there—for him. You should probably stick with the burger."

She laughed. "Thanks, and thanks for your help."

"Glad to do it." He started toward his truck again, tossing off a friendly wave. "Nice to have met you. Both of you."

"You, too, from both of us." She took the dog's paw and waved it.

He opened the driver's side door to climb in, then paused and leaned inside the cab, as if looking for something.

"That right there—" she whispered with her cheek pressed against the animal's head "—is the whole reason I came back to Baconburg."

She didn't mean the man. She meant the man's willingness to take time out of his own schedule to help a stranger. Okay, Polly could not lie, even to herself— maybe the man…a little. Or a man like him. What Polly really wanted in Baconburg was the life she had always dreamed possible, and that included a good man and her own family that would stay together no matter what.

Before she could shuffle the little dog into the backseat of her car, the animal dashed around the back of the car. Polly glanced back and there was Sam walking across her front yard, heading back toward her. And he had his hand up in a wave. She raised her hand as the dog returned and ducked into the back of the car.

"Wow, maybe I do mean *that* guy is the reason I came here," she whispered to her canine companion as she took in a sharp breath. "He sure seems like he isn't ready for me to go yet."

The dog paced back and forth over the seat. If she kept him, she knew she'd have to invest in a safety restraint but thought for now this was safer than leaving him in her house or outside.

"Maybe I should see if he wants to join us for burgers." Polly gripped the door.

Sam came to a halt in her yard. His raised hand fell to his side.

She smiled and worked up the courage to say, "Hi, it looks like you're thinking what I'm thinking…"

He cocked his head and narrowed his eyes. "That your dog has my hat?"

"Your… Oh, no! You set it on the driveway, didn't you?" She glanced back in time to see the animal give the hat a shake. "No!"

Sam put his thumb and forefinger to the bridge of his nose. Probably unable to look at what the dog had done.

"I am so sorry." She hurried to the back door, reached in and grabbed the hat by the brim. It took a firm tug to rescue it, but she held it out to him.

He looked down, his expression guarded.

Polly stared at the damp brim and the crown the dog had shaken into a shapeless wonder. "I'm so sorry," she said again. Her voice was barely a whisper.

"What's done is done." Finally he put his own hand up and turned his head to one side as if to say, *I don't want it now.* "It's okay. Don't feel bad. It was just an old Christmas gift from my wife."

"Wife?" Now she felt careless and a bit silly. "I didn't think you were—"

"My *late* wife," he clarified. He frowned down at

the mash up of brim and crown. "Hmm. Well, okay, then. I guess that's the end of that."

He flicked it with one finger as if to say, *Goodbye, old friend,* then raised his hand in a sort of salute to her, turned and headed for his truck.

"Your taking this so well only makes me feel worse," she called after him. "Isn't there something I can do with it?"

"Maybe we can cut ear holes in it and let the dog wear it." He didn't look back.

Polly climbed into the car and looked her only friend in all of Baconburg in the eye. Poor little thing. Of all of God's creatures, he could understand her fear, sadness, embarrassment and loneliness when she said, "Maybe Essie was right. Maybe running away isn't going to be the big solution to my problems that I thought it would be."

Chapter Two

"So, let me get this straight." Sam's sister, Gina, slipped off her computer glasses and aimed her sharp-eyed gaze at him. "You just left your hat in her hands and drove off?"

"Hey, it wasn't like I was going to wear it home." Sam moved around the kitchen table gathering up the three empty bowls where a few minutes ago his daughters had been eating ice cream. He stacked Juliette's "sprinkles, please, Daddy, and no nuts" dish inside Hayley's "chocolate on chocolate with a side of chocolate" one. Finally he took up Caroline's "whatever you give me is fine, Daddy" dish, held them up and said to his sister, "Anyone who thinks those girls are completely identical has never had to feed them."

"Don't try to change the subject on me." Gina wriggled in the high-backed oak chair, then kicked it up on two legs, bracing her hiking shoe against the table leg to stabilize herself. "Marie gave you that hat."

"I am well aware." Sam plunked the bowls into the sink. He turned on the water to rinse them out and said, loudly enough to be heard over the splashing,

"By the way, if Mom were here she'd tell you she didn't care if you are the owner of this place now, you keep both your feet and all the chair legs on the floor, young lady."

Gina rocked the chair slightly and crossed her arms defiantly, not even flinching when her long, dark blond braid got snagged under one arm. "Tell me again who this woman is."

"Mom?" He faked surprise to cover his determination not to prolong any discussion of Polly Bennett. "I know she and Dad have been living in Florida for a few years now, but—"

"You know who I mean. The mysterious woman who got you to help rescue a dog. A dog, Sam. That's huge for you."

He finished washing up the dishes, then moved to drying them off with the towel that usually hung from the handle of the oven door. "I don't dislike dogs and she's not mysterious. Her name is Polly Bennett from Atlanta, Georgia."

"New in town?"

"Didn't say." He put the bowls up and shut the cabinet, wishing he could finish up this conversation that easily. He wouldn't normally have even mentioned any of this to Gin, but she had asked if he had left his hat at work when he'd come home. And when she didn't get an answer had wondered aloud if he had left it in her truck and she'd have to get it out of there later. She wouldn't let it go, even several hours later.

"You don't suppose this Polly Bennett is the new schoolteacher?" Gina asked.

"Thought of that myself." But he'd dismissed it

almost instantly. Polly Bennett, with her wild, dark hair, her fresh face and pint-size stature, didn't look like any grade-school teacher he'd ever had. "But then I remembered you said word on the grapevine was they'd gone with someone born here in Baconburg."

"That's right." The chair legs came clunking down. She shifted her laptop around on the table as if she was about to get back to work promoting the farm's upcoming fall pumpkin-themed festival, the Pumpkin Jump, online. Instead she looked up at him again. "And you just left your hat with a stranger?"

"Stop this ride." He held up his hands. "I am not going around again."

"Fine." She leaned in over her keyboard and put her fingers over the touch pad. But always one to want the last word, she said, "You know, they say if you leave something at a person's house, it's a subconscious way of giving yourself an excuse to go back."

"Then *they* don't know me because I don't *go* back." He headed out the kitchen door into the hallway.

"Walking away is not the same as moving forward, you know."

"I'm not walking away. I'm going to check on the girls and tell them good-night." He paused at the bottom of the stairs.

"Good luck with that."

"I don't believe in luck. I believe in God's blessings." He wasn't sure why he'd said it, but the words, and thinking of the woman who had said them, actually made him smile.

"Fine, go say good-night to your little blessings. Remember they're all wired up about getting their classroom assignments tomorrow. I hope you're ready to deal with the fallout."

"I was born ready." Whatever came his way, Sam met it, wrestled with it, made it his or left it behind. Nothing slowed him down. Full speed ahead. Farm kid. College football hero. Hometown business owner. Husband. Father. Widower. Single dad to three six-year-old girls.

He moved forward, always forward, tackling every new role with his faith to uphold him. When he made up his mind, applied his experience and attitude, he could handle anything.

Except second grade.

Sam took a deep breath, stepped into the doorway of the room shared by his daughters and made one loud clap of his hands. "Big day tomorrow, girls! Second-grade registration and we find out who your new teachers will be."

"There's only *one* new teacher," Hayley, the most outspoken of the three, reminded him.

As if he needed reminding. Three second-grade classes at Van Buren Elementary, three Goodacre girls aching for a chance to be teacher's pet to somebody who *hadn't* known them since they were toddlers. A school with a policy not to put multiples in the same classroom, and one new teacher. He didn't have to be a math whiz to know he was going to have a couple of upset girls tomorrow, maybe for a big part of the whole school year.

"Okay, let's not borrow trouble." Especially not triple trouble, he thought. "We'll deal with whoever gets the new teacher the way we deal with everything. And how's that?"

"With grace and with gratitude, with a never-give-up attitude." The trio repeated in unison another line from the bedtime stories their mother had created, stories that they each knew by heart.

He thought of Marie saying those same words, and on the heels of that, he thought of the cowboy-hat Christmas gift she'd given him as a joke. No one expected him to wear it. Which was why Sam had put it on the day they moved out to the farm, a month after Marie had died. He'd worn it every day since. It was his way of making himself embrace change. Now…

In the blink of an eye, his mind went to Polly Bennett. *Polly.*

What a great name. Fit her, too. Upbeat. Fresh, yet maybe a little old-fashioned. And a good heart. He'd seen it in her from the moment their eyes met until she looked at him with true regret over ruining his hat.

Unpredictable, too, just like that crazy hair of hers. Sam had had to clench his fingers tight a couple of time to keep from brushing it out of her eyes. Then that whole deal with that little lost dog…

That thought snapped Sam back into the moment. He shifted his boots on the old farmhouse floorboards. His mind did not usually skip the tracks like that. He had to get ahold of himself. "Actually, I meant that we'd meet the problem head-on and not look back because…"

"The rest of our life is ahead of us." Hayley and Juliette repeated one of the many mottoes Sam had taught them. Caroline just looked at him, saying nothing.

"That's right. Never look back." He didn't just talk the talk in this case. Sam had made these past few years about demonstrating those traits to his girls. People had told him he kept the girls too busy and spent too little time making a new life for himself.

He knew what they meant by that. They thought Sam needed to fall in love again. What those people didn't understand was that he had made up his mind that all his time and energy had to go into his girls, into making sure they did not miss out on anything because they were missing their mom. Maybe one day he'd be able to let up a little and meet…someone. But that certainly wasn't going to be tomorrow. Tomorrow presented its own problems. "Now say your prayers and go to bed."

He reached along the wall and flicked off the light, but instead of turning around and leaving the girls to do what was expected of them, he lingered to listen as they thanked God for their day, their home, the food they ate and then began the list of the people they loved.

"Bless Daddy." Always the leader, Hayley's request came clear and firm.

"And bless Uncle Max," Hayley's carbon copy, Juliette, chimed in to add the youngest of Sam's siblings.

"And bless Aunt Gina." Caroline tacked on a request on behalf of Sam's sister.

"And also, if You don't mind…" Hayley started again, her tone uncharacteristically tentative. "If Mommy is close by to You in heaven right now…"

Don't look back... Sam wanted to plead with his child, *Let your mother go and don't dwell on the loss.* A lump rose in his throat, which he pushed down again. He turned away. No point in standing there having his heart tugged toward a past he could not change. His life…more importantly, his daughters' lives, lay ahead of them and he had to keep fixed on that and never stop moving forward. It was the only way they could survive.

"If Mom is there with You," Juliette took over for her sister, her tone bright and cheerful, "give her a hug from us."

Sam froze in the dim hallway.

And finally Caroline added softly, "And tell her we will never forget her."

Sam dragged air into his lungs, ignoring the dull ache that still caught him by surprise even two years after his wife's death. Maybe *pain* was the wrong word. *Emptiness? Sadness?* He didn't know anymore. He'd made his peace with his loss, accepted it as God's will and got on with normal life for his girls' sake.

That's why he had moved them from the house he and his wife, Marie, had owned in their small town out to the family farm his sister had taken over from their parents. He did it to show the girls how life was about change and growth. What better place to show that than a farm? Were they not getting it? What more could he do?

"And bless the new teacher, whoever gets her." This time Hayley led off. "I hope she's fun and smart and nice."

Again a twinge of emotion, only this time it was not grief but a mix of misgivings.

"And it wouldn't be bad if she also thinks triplets are cool. And also if she's pretty—" Juliette turned her head enough to peer over her shoulder through one half-opened eye "—and not married."

It hit Sam like a sucker punch. This was why he needed to stop listening in on his girls' prayers, because he did not want the girls using their prayer time to try to make a point to him. It didn't matter if the teacher was pretty or single—all he cared about was how she would help whichever daughter landed in her classroom to have a successful school year.

"What did you say?" He put his hand to the side of his head to remind them he was standing right there within earshot.

"Amen," Hayley concluded.

"Amen," the others agreed.

"Go to bed," Sam muttered, his hand on the doorknob. Just before he pulled it closed, he leaned in to add, "And tomorrow don't make me remind you of my own personal set of no-no's."

"We know. Dad, we know all about your no-no's." Hayley sighed, got to her feet and threw back the covers on her single bed. "No dogs."

That sounded particularly harsh all of a sudden after helping Polly Bennett wrangle that sweet little lost dog. But they had imposed enough on his sister's time by moving in. To add pet care while he ran and remodeled Downtown Drug and while the girls were in school, and dance classes and tumbling and T-ball... just wasn't fair.

"It's not the 'no dogs' rule I'm talking about," he reminded them. "No…"

Juliette and then Caroline rose, each flipping back the covers on their own beds, too.

Three little sighs and three sets of eyes—probably rolling in irritation as they climbed into their beds.

"And no…" he prompted one more time.

"No matchmaking," they all said as one. Then one, two, three, they pulled up their covers in a way that made Sam think of cartoon princesses flouncing off in a huff.

"That's right. Good night, sweethearts." He gave them a nod and turned to shut the door at last, but just before he pulled it closed, he heard one of those little princesses mutter an addendum to his hard-and-fast no-matchmaking rule.

"For now."

Ready? Had he thought he was ready? Oh, no. He was not ready for this. Not ready at all.

Chapter Three

Early that next morning, Polly hurried to the school, still feeling badly about the whole hat thing. With that weighing on her mind, she didn't even feel like chattering out loud to her canine passenger as she drove the four blocks from her house to the place where her street, Mills, met Main. At the intersection, governed only by a four-way stop sign, she took a moment to read the official signs.

"Baconburg Business District." She glanced toward the road that she knew wound around toward the highway where a chain hotel, a couple of fast-food places and a mega grocery store dotted the landscape.

She took a peek down at a patchwork of buildings that told the story of a town that had known growth spurts and setbacks. Polly smiled. "Baconburg Historic District, which means the cool stuff is thataway."

But Polly was headed straight down Mills to the school and she couldn't linger any longer. She sighed. "Too bad there isn't a hat-blocking place back there."

Oblivious, the dog bounced right to left, then right again. In a few minutes she pulled into the school parking lot. The only other cars seemed to belong to the staff.

Today was the day the students would be finding out whose classroom they would be assigned to. The principal had okayed her coming in to collect some supplies but had asked that Polly not stick around to avoid "complications." Polly understood the code word for school politics. She knew that as a fairly new teacher—just three years out of college—and totally new to Van Buren Elementary, some parents would have misgivings about their kids being assigned to her. Others would demand to have their children in Miss Bennett's class, thinking she would have fresher perspective, all the latest approaches and no preconceptions about which were the good kids and which were the "problems." Though Polly couldn't really imagine how much of a problem your average small-town second grader could be.

"No more problem than you right now, mister." She whirred the window down a few inches, got out and shut the door. She started to turn toward the front door of the single-level blond-brick building, then suddenly felt compelled to explain, "You just have to stay here for two minutes while I run into my classroom here to get some paper. I can make up flyers there so we can find your parents, okay?"

The thick tail thumped against the back of the seat and he whimpered softly as if to tell her he understood.

She tapped the window. Did she really have to make flyers today? She had moved here to learn to take her time, relish the past and not be so anxious to press forward, after all.

A silvery-blue minivan came gliding up past her car and pulled up to the curb in front of her.

Parents were beginning to arrive. She had two choices. Go inside and get what she came for and get out. Or run away.

The passenger door of the minivan swung open and Polly couldn't help taking a peek.

One little girl with a bright red ponytail, dressed in canvas-colored overalls over a lime-green camp shirt scrambled out onto the sidewalk with so much energy that she almost fell over herself. No, that wasn't herself she had fallen over. It was…

"Twins!" Polly couldn't help it. She whispered the word in a rush of excitement to the little dog.

The second child emerged. Her red hair was woven into a gorgeous French braid tied with a pink ribbon. In fact, everything she wore was pink. Pink top, pink skirt, pink sparkly shoelaces in pink sequined tennis shoes.

Polly laughed out loud at the sight. "A set of identical—"

A third child climbed out.

"Triplets," Polly murmured.

This one wore tennis shoes, too, plain white ones. With faded jeans and an ill-fitting gray shirt. Her hair was caught up in pigtails, the right one a good two inches higher than the left.

That was the one that got to Polly. She felt a smile start that grew beyond simple amusement to recognition of a kindred spirit. All three girls turned and looked at her, their eyes wide.

Polly wondered if she should say hello. It seemed

wrong to just get in her car and rush off now. Maybe she should wave and say, *See ya soon, I hope.* Or should she ask their names? Before she could speak or move or even make up her mind, the driver's door swung open.

"I told you girls we were leaving too early. I don't know if the doors are even open yet." A large, weathered cowboy boot hit the concrete followed by more than six feet of tall, muscular man.

Polly leaned back against the car, a bit for support, a bit to give her room to take in the whole view. "You!"

"Me!" Sam grinned as he shut his door and started toward her. "So, you have a kid in this school, too?"

"Too?" Polly looked at the children, then at the van and realized nobody else was getting out.

He pointed toward the girls each in turn. "Hayley, Juliette and Caroline."

"Those are...*your* daughters?" Sam Goodacre had identical triplets. Some women might have wanted to run from a situation like that, but for Polly, just seeing these girls made her feel less homesick for her own twin.

"Yeah." He held up three fingers. "All mine. And you..."

Three high-pitched squeals tore through the quiet air of the summer morning.

"You...brought...a dog." They all sang out a variation of almost the same thing.

"I don't have any kids, Sam. I'm not even married." Polly moved closer to him to speak softly enough that the girls wouldn't hear as she whispered her confession, "I'm the new teacher."

"Of course you are." He shook his head. "You are the single, new teacher with an adorable, homeless puppy."

In a flash of red curls and giggles, the girls ran up to the car. The puppy rushed to the side and licked the place where the small hands pressed against the glass.

"You say 'new teacher' like it's a bad thing." She ducked her head to try to meet his lowered gaze. "It's because of the hat thing, right? It's the hat?"

"Forget about the hat. That's the past." He waved his hand as if actually pushing it behind them. "No, it's more complicated than that, starting with the fact that my girls are starting second grade this year. This is Hayley. That one is Juliette." He pointed to each girl as he spoke. "And that is Caroline."

"Oh." Polly whipped around and saw the girls in another light—not as fellow multiples but each a potential student.

The one Sam called Caroline gasped, her eyes grew wide and in that second there was a light in her to rival her other sisters' natural vivaciousness. Caroline turned her head to tell Polly, "I like your dog."

"He's not mine, really." She slipped away from Sam and went to the children. "I found him hanging around my house. I'm going to put up flyers to see if I can find his real owners."

"You don't have to do that. *I* know his real owners." Caroline jerked her head around to fix her huge, pleading eyes on her father.

"Me, too." Juliette ran to the car to peer inside.

"Me, too, too," Hayley said with sweetness but conviction.

Sam strode forward from the parking lot to the sidewalk, motioning the girls away from the car. "Okay, girls, you know the rules."

"We weren't matchmaking, Dad," they all protested together in perfect harmony, a trick only identical multiples could fully pull off.

"Matchmaking?" Polly laughed, a bit too nervously for her own comfort. What was this all about? Sam had a rule against matchmaking?

Sam scowled. "I meant the rule about dogs."

"Oh, so we *can* matchmake?" Hayley rushed forward.

"No." He spread his hands wide as if calling a runner out at home plate.

Polly felt a blush rush from the constriction in her chest to the tips of her ears. She didn't know if she should say something or get out of there fast.

"You know we can't have a dog right now. You have too many activities. Juliette, you want to give up ballet?"

The girl opened her mouth, but before she could actually give an answer, the man moved on, intent on making his point quick and clean. It was a familiar means of "communicating" in her family and it made Polly tense up.

"And, Hayley, you have your hands full with your 4-H projects, right?"

Hayley put her shoulders back and didn't answer—a means of getting her message across that Sam did not seem to notice.

"And, Caroline…well, when school starts I'm sure you'll find some things to keep you busy. We're all busy. Bringing a dog into our lives now wouldn't be fair to your aunt Gina having to care for it, or to the dog not getting our full attention."

Caroline glanced back and the dog. "But…"

"We don't even know." Sam tried to glower at the girls then at the dog, but he didn't quite pull it off. "This dog may belong to someone."

"He does belong to someone, Daddy, to *us*," Caroline insisted in such a plaintive voice that Polly could feel the longing in her own bones.

"No." Sam's insistence told a story of something more going on than his simplistic explanation. "He is not ours."

"He should be ours," Hayley said firmly.

"He could be ours." Juliette spoke a bit more tentatively.

Caroline fixed her eyes on her father and added, "If Mama was alive, he *would* be ours."

Sam pressed his lips into a thin white line.

Maybe she was overly sensitive because she'd been so lonely last night, or because she felt so guilty about Sam's hat, or maybe because she honestly liked Sam and felt a connection to his daughters. Whatever the reason, Polly couldn't stay quiet another minute. She hurried to the driver's side door, her keys jangling in her hand.

"You know," Polly said as she rushed to his rescue and put the key in the lock, "I think I'll just take care of him until we find out if someone is looking for him. Right now I've got to go. The teachers aren't supposed to be here when the kids and parents start to show up. Bye, girls, it was so nice to meet you."

someone who wouldn't hesitate to take in a lost
an animal she might have to give back if the real
ers showed up? I can't put my kids through that."
Then let them have their own dog, like lots of kids
age do." Max sifted through the plans and pencils
tered on a makeshift table in the soon-to-be lunch-
nter area of the store.

Sam's throat constricted just enough to strain his
rds as he shot back, "Lots of kids their age haven't
ffered the kind of loss my girls have."

"Did you ever think it might be good for them to
ave a dog to take care of, not to mention a nice lady
their life—in your life?" Max took up a pencil and
cked it behind his ear. "It might help them find a new
ind of normal."

"There's a piece of the puzzle you're not seeing."
am turned and headed back through the store. Time
get this subject and this day back on track. "This
g she's found could be the model for the dog in those
dtime stories Marie used to tell the girls."

"The ones Gina has written up and wants to pub-
sh?"

"The triplets have grown up with an idealized ver-
on of an adorable little dog who never gets sick, never
ts old, never…" Sam gave a thumbs-down gesture
ther than say what he meant. He met Max's gaze and
ve his final word on the matter. "No dog could live
to the one in their imagination. It wouldn't be fair
the animal."

Sam headed back to the pharmacy.

Max moved around the work space, putting him-
f in a place to make sure Sam could hear him as he

The girls all groaned.

Sam mouthed a thank-you that made her feel good
and a little sad at the same time. How she longed
to point out those missed clues with the girls. Why
wouldn't he allow them to have a dog? And the no-
matchmaking deal?

Suddenly instead of seeing a funny, kind man of
faith she perceived the hurt he hid even from himself.

As she drove away from the family scene, her gaze
fell on the hat that she had left in the car last night. She
couldn't talk rules or matchmaking with Sam, couldn't
interfere with his parenting, but she could help him out
here. She could do everything within her power to get
this puppy back to his real home so that she could give
the dog and the girls a happy ending. But to do that she
had to act fast.

"You know, for someone who came to Baconburg
to slow down the pace of her life—" she told her passenger, who woofed softly in response "—I sure have
been in an awful big hurry ever since I met that Sam
Goodacre."

"So?" Sam's younger brother, Max, called out the
second Sam came blowing through the back door of
Downtown Drug.

He had taken the girls back to the farm after they'd
gotten their class assignments. The whole process had
taken longer than he'd expected and he was late getting in to open the store. The girls had actually taken
their assignments pretty well. Hayley and Juliette pat-
ting Caroline on the back as a kind of congratulations,

even, and saying they didn't mind. Until they learned just who the new teacher was.

Sam had met the cries of "unfair" and pleas for him to go to the school and let them all be in Miss Bennett's class with his usual "let's not let this slow us down" answers, which hadn't helped much. Maybe it was because for the first time in a long time, he hadn't really believed his own proclamations. In finding out Polly had this connection to his children, it wasn't just the two girls in the other classes that felt just a little bit cheated.

"So?" Max's voice rang out again. "Just how cute is this new teacher?"

The first thing Sam encountered was the last thing he had the time or patience to put up with.

"I spoke with her for five whole minutes in front of the school this morning." Sam slipped the long white lab coat he kept hanging on the door of the pharmacist's station over his street clothes. He strode farther into the old store where his little brother, Max, stood amid a disarray of power tools, how-to manuals and a row of still-crated restaurant-grade appliances. "Do not tell me it's all over town already?"

"Hey, you belly crawl across the new lady in town's driveway one evening, then get spotted talking to her in front of the school the next day?" Max grinned his famous cocky grin, and gave an unconvincing shrug. "People are gonna talk."

"She's Caroline's teacher." In Sam's mind that was the end of the discussion. He moved on toward the front door, flipping on display lights and setting things in their rightful spots.

"So?" Max called after him, not [...] as an inch to help prep the place for [...]

So. Max had a way of asking som[...] had no way of formulating an answer [...]

"Look, it's Baconburg. Everyone [...] teacher or scout leader or church youth [...] or cousin or… You get it. As long as you [...] on the up-and-up and don't give anyone rea[...] cern vis-à-vis the whole teacher-as-a-role-m[...] I think you could manage a few dates with [...]

Sam gripped the door's ice-cold metal ha[...] the chill sank through all the way to his finge[...] clenched his jaw and looked out at the town wh[...] had grown up, the place that had cheered hi[...] youthful triumphs and embraced him in his [...] deepest grief. He had fully prepared for his [...] this town to sustain him as he raised his girls [...] grew up and had their own triumphs. That [...] his sole priority.

Then he'd seen Polly Bennett trying to re[...] stray dog from under her car and for a split s[...] whole life hit Pause.

"She takes in strays," he said loud enoug[...] to hear, but not so much for Max's benefit. "[...] sad-eyed, not-too-great-smelling strays."

"Great. That means you might actual[...] chance with her."

"Very funny." He glanced back and laug[...] brotherly jab. Max had always been the la[...] of the Goodacre boys, so Sam could under[...] Max's mind would immediately jump to th[...] conclusion. "But really, how could I ever ge[...]

folded his burly arms over his broad chest and asked, "Have you noticed, big bro, that every time you give an excuse for not letting the girls have a dog, it changes a little?"

"I have work to do." Sam stood still for a moment, aware that Max had a point but that he also didn't have any say in Sam's life. "You have heard of that, right? Work?"

Max withdrew the pencil and a tumble of his shaggy, sun-streaked hair stuck out over his tanned ear. "Hey, I'm working on this."

"If that were true we'd have an operational lunch counter by now." Sam didn't mean to sound mad, but he'd reached his limit on this subject today. No dog. No matchmaking with Polly Bennett. Why couldn't anyone get that? "You know they call it a lunch counter because people expect to come in, sit at the counter and get served a hot, quick lunch, right? Not because everyone is counting the days until this project eats your lunch and you take off again."

"You know you sound like a grouchy old man, don't you?" Max laughed. "Go count pills."

"I will. And while I'm doing that, can you handle taking care of the store? I do not need to be disturbed any more today."

"Any more? You're saying something…or someone…has already disturbed your tightly wound little world, bro?" Max chuckled. "Good for her. If she's as cute as they say, good for you, too. It's about time."

Chapter Four

Getting her supplies from the school wasn't going to work for her flyer project. Polly had taken her wriggling little wet-nosed charge back to her house and settled him in, then headed out to try to find a place to buy more paper. When she found herself at that crossroads between the Historic and Business districts of Baconburg again, she didn't hesitate.

A few minutes later she was strolling down the sidewalk, soaking in every small detail of the lovely old historic buildings. Nothing was going to hurry her along again today. Brass fixtures, ornate cement trimwork, even the names of the old establishments spelled out in colored tile in the entryways leading to the doors. Try as she might she could not recall any of this from her childhood. She strongly suspected that her parents preferred to do their shopping someplace shiny and sophisticated, upscale and urban. She paused just outside her destination, a sweet little throwback to an earlier time, Downtown Drug.

She blinked at the image of a black-haired, dreamy-eyed young woman reflected back at her. She could easily imagine herself in a pillbox hat and gloves, proper Miss Bennett, grammar-school teacher, strolling downtown circa 1950. How could her family have not loved this town? How could they have run so fast and so far away from it?

If Polly didn't look just like her sister, Essie, who so clearly belonged with the Bennett family, Polly would have wondered if she had been switched at birth. All of historic Baconburg, right down to the blue-, white- and silver-painted plateglass windows of Downtown Drug put a whole new spring in Polly's step. She crossed over the threshold of the front door and felt as if she'd walked into another time, a sweeter time, a time when people made time for one another.

She stole a moment to take in the black-and-white-tiled floors, sunny-yellow walls and shelves filled with every sort of thing a person might need. The old store still had a gleaming wooden checkout stand, with a shiny computerized scanner and cash register attached. That didn't dampen Polly's enthusiasm for the quaintness of the old place. She could just imagine how for so many years people in Baconburg must have come here for the things they needed—medicine, candy, school supplies and who knew what else.

"Welcome to Downtown Drug. We've got whatever your little heart desires." A warm, deep masculine voice called out from somewhere unseen in the store. "If you need help finding it, I'm back here at the lunch counter."

"A lunch counter." Polly sighed. "This I've got to see!"

She wound her way back toward the friendly voice,

expecting to find a nice paunchy, slightly balding middle-aged man wearing a white bib apron getting a big grill ready for the day's business.

"Hello?" she called out. She rounded the end of a row of shelves and stopped inches from a pile of red vinyl benches and tables that must have once been booths. Beyond that a bright yellow strip of plastic, the kind she'd seen around crime scenes marked off an area filled with power tools, sawdust and chaos.

Middle-aged? Maybe if the average life expectancy was around sixty. Balding? Not even slightly. Her gaze moved from the shoulder-length waves of light brown hair topped with sun-washed blond streaks to his tanned face and two- or three-day growth of beard. He wore a chain around his neck with a cross on it, and a faded T-shirt rolled up at the sleeves to reveal bulging biceps.

He smiled. "Hey there, pretty lady. You got a question? I don't actually work in the store, so I'm not sure where you'd find that. If you'd like, I can ask the old man."

He raised his voice on the last two words and directed them toward the raised platform framed in black-painted wood with sliding glass-panel windows and *Pharmacy* lettered in gold.

In response, one of the panels slid almost closed.

The man in front of her burst out laughing. "They do get cranky when they get old, don't they?"

"I like older people," Polly said in the unseen man's defense. "And I like older places. I think it's a shame you're tearing up this wonderful old piece of local history. Please tell me you're not going to install one of those fast-food kiosks like they have in quick markets and all over the airport in Atlanta."

"Atlanta! You're…" He pointed at her and his face lit up like a kid's at Christmas.

"I'm what?"

"From Atlanta," he said as if that was what he had been reacting to—and fairly unconvincingly, too.

What did this construction worker in surfer dude's clothing know about her? Should she be uneasy or flattered?

"Maybe I should talk to that *old man*." She turned and skirted sideways, keenly aware of the smiling carpenter's eyes on her. Even when she heard the squeak of a door, she did not turn toward the pharmacist's station. Her gaze locked on the other man, she raised the piece of paper. "I have a list. I just need to get in, get out and get back to getting this little dog I found back where he belongs."

"I thought you were keeping the dog."

Polly gasped at the sound of Sam's voice. The slip of paper with her supply list on it slid through her fingers, flipped in the air and fell between her feet and Sam's cowboy boots.

"I can't… That is…*you* convinced me…" Polly looked at him, her mouth open. Sam Goodacre. The guy who showed up in her driveway. Then at the school. Now… "I can't believe we keep running into each other."

"Welcome to life in a small town. The upside is that you tend to make a tight-knit circle of friends and associates who are always there for each other. The downside is that you have a tight-knit circle of friends and associates and they're always *there* for each other, whether you want them there or not."

She thought of her life in Atlanta where she barely knew anyone in her building, or even her church. Where her job meant she rarely worked with the same people more than a few days in a row, and even so, half the time they rarely had time to make eye contact. Of course, not everyone in the city was like that, but that had been her experience and so... "I didn't say I didn't like it."

"Oh?" He tipped his head to one side. "I guess sometimes it *is* kinda nice."

Her heart fluttered. She took a breath and held it just long enough until she noticed her head felt light. She let her words rush out in a whisper, "What are you doing here?"

"I own the place. Bought out my father-in-law when he retired last year." He stuck his thumb under the name tag on his white lab coat, closing the already-too-close distance between them with the starched white fabric.

Polly pressed her lips together to keep from actually reading the tag aloud as she tried to ignore how this man's nearness made her so aware of everything from the rasp of his coat over his shirt to the pounding of her pulse in her temples.

"You're..." She glanced over her shoulder in the direction of the lunch counter. "You're the old man?"

He chuckled softly. "I see you've met my brother, Max."

"Your brother..." Suddenly the guy seeming to know something about her made sense. It also made her wonder if it was Sam who had told his brother about her, and just what Sam might have said. Never in her life had she had this kind of instantaneous reaction to a man. Just being around him filled her with anticipation and the expectation that something good was coming her way. She liked that. Liked him. A good guy. A good dad. A Christian and…

"I thought you were a farmer."

"Close. I'm a pharmacist." He walked over to the raised platform and slid the glass back to reveal a plaque with all his credentials engraved under his name. "I just live on a farm."

"But the truck I first saw you in…"

"Belongs to our family farm. My sister and I trade off depending on our cargo. Her organic produce gets the truck, my redheaded progeny get the minivan."

She couldn't help smiling. "Those girls seem like pretty precious cargo to me."

"Yeah, they are." He nodded as if he really appreciated her saying that, then suddenly his brow furrowed. "Did you come in here for something special?"

"Oh! My list!" She bent immediately to retrieve the list.

"Let me…" Sam did the same.

They both reached out. Polly clenched her jaw, bracing herself for that dull, painful, embarrassing head clunk. Surprised when it didn't come, she jerked her head up.

He was standing there, his face inches from hers. In the space of a heartbeat she lost herself in those caring brown eyes.

"I'll just get…" she murmured.

"Here, let me…" he said at the same time.

Both bent slightly forward, hands extended and faces close. Static electricity in the very air drew a strand of Polly's hair toward his. For a split second, if anyone had caught a glimpse of them with those words on their lips and their gazes entwined, they might have thought they were just about to kiss.

"Um, I have to go." Polly jerked her body upright and raked her curled fingers through her hair, pulling it back into place. "I left the dog and…I have to go."

She didn't wait for an answer, just spun on her heel and ran. For an instant she listened for his footsteps behind her, or for him to call for her not to leave. Not a sound, not as she fled with her face flushed and her throat tight, not as she hit the door and pushed her way out onto the sidewalk.

In the glass storefront she no longer imagined the daydream of prim Miss Bennett but saw herself. Polly, who wanted to find her place in the world but who never quite fit in had just met a man who made her feel as if anything was possible—except a match made between the two of them.

Sam couldn't get the near kiss out of his mind the rest of the day. Thoughts of Polly Bennett popped up uninvited in the seconds between the phone ringing and his answering it. Could it be her calling about whatever she had come in to get from the store?

Her image formed slowly in his thoughts as he walked by the spot where Polly had stood. When he caught the whiff of sawdust and bubblegum, the scent in the store surrounding them earlier. So it pulled him up short when, shortly after four, his sister came in to deliver the triplets to him and his brother simultaneously made an announcement.

"All right! Gina's here." Max clapped his hands together, then swung his legs over the tarp-covered lunch counter. "I'm off."

Hayley clambered up onto one of the dozen stools planted around the covered counter. Juliette went on tiptoe, gave a twirl and took the seat next to her. Sam reached out to help Caroline climb up to another stool, frowning at his brother as he asked, "Where you going, Max?"

"To pay a visit to that pretty new teacher."

"Why?"

"Because she came in here this morning with a list of things she needed and after two minutes in your presence she ran out of here without getting any of it." The small rectangle of paper caught between Max's fingers crackled. "So I thought I'd do the neighborly thing—fill her list and take it over to her."

"We want to go." Hayley spoke for all three girls.

"I have a motorcycle, girls. One of you can ride behind me and one on my shoulders, but the other one…" He squinted at Sam. The girls understood this was just another example of Uncle Max's outrageous humor, but Sam recognized the challenge in his younger brother's tone. He was baiting Sam. "You got a skateboard and some clothesline in this place?"

"Very funny." Sam met that challenge with his feet planted firmly in front of his daughters, on the floor of his place of business. He wasn't going to let his younger brother goad him into getting riled up about

Polly Bennett. That no-matchmaking rule did not just apply to the triplets.

Max made an exaggeratedly casual shrug, ending with both hands held out as if weighing the two options. "Somebody's got to stay here. Somebody needs to take these to the lovely Miss Bennett."

"Dad can do it," Caroline volunteered, because they clearly all knew Sam wasn't going to speak up for himself.

Max gave a big ol' self-satisfied grin. "Why didn't I think of that?"

Sam opened his mouth to launch into an explanation of his special set of rules to Max, then reconsidered. It wasn't as if Max ever listened to the rules, anyway.

"How about Gina?" Sam fixed his gaze on his sister, who had paused long enough at the counter to drop some change into the drawer and sell herself a pack of gum. "It would be perfect. You take the girls and deliver this stuff to—"

"Sorry." She leaned down, rummaged around under the counter, then popped back up holding Sam's spare truck keys. "I have an appointment with a seed catalog."

As soon as Gina reached the door, she pitched Sam the keys to the minivan. "See you tonight."

The keys hit the floor with a metallic clank.

Max bent down to scoop them up and dangled them in front of Sam. "I can hold down the store while you pay a visit."

"I don't want the girls getting attached to that dog," Sam muttered through clenched teeth, not from anger but from trying to disguise the sentiment from his daughters.

"Fine. They can stay with me." He pressed the cluster of keys into Sam's palm. "I could use the girls' help picking out paint colors."

"Green!" Hayley jumped in the air.

"Pink!" Juliette gave a twirl.

"Can you use wallpaper?" Caroline squinted at the wall as if already taking mental measurements for the job.

The girls threw themselves into the assignment with the kind of enthusiasm that only a chance to do an end run around their dad's no-matchmaking rule could inspire.

What was he going to do about it? Haul the girls over there and risk their falling in love with that little lost pup? Or send his brother over to Polly Bennett's house and risk her falling in love with his hound dog of a brother? That shouldn't matter, but…

He sighed, snagged the bag with the goods gathered up by Max and headed for the door. "I'll be back in an hour. I'm going to make a delivery."

Chapter Five

Sam pulled the family minivan into Polly's driveway, took one look at his surroundings and groaned. They'd done it. Right under his nose. Despite all the so-called rules he laid out and his own insistence he wouldn't be falling for any of their shenanigans, Sam had played right into the matchmaking hands of Max and the triplets.

"I can't believe I fell for that," he muttered quietly, realizing now that Max had never even asked where Polly lived.

He chuckled softly at the ingenuity of the foursome, even if their matchmaking mission was doomed to failure. He was making a delivery. That was all. He focused on the task at hand, getting these things to a customer, to Caroline's teacher. No distractions, no complications.

"No problem." Sam couldn't believe the words coming out of his own mouth not ten seconds after he had knocked on the door and Polly had asked him to come around to the back of the house, go down through the basement door and up into the house because she didn't want the little dog to run out the door again. He should have just hollered back through the closed door that he'd leave the things on the front porch, have a nice day, see you around, something like that. Instead he took the long way around, into the basement, up the stairs and through the door that let him into the small, sunny kitchen.

The impact of what he had just done hit him. Kitchens were generally considered the heart of the home, weren't they? He was in the heart of Polly territory. And he liked it.

Of course, the same neighbors who had seen him on his belly in Polly's driveway might just have taken notice of his going around the back way and letting himself into the new schoolteacher's…make that the pretty, single, new schoolteacher's…house. He wasn't just standing on the porch as he usually would do for a delivery. He wasn't even standing in the front room where the two of them could be seen through the big front window, not that the people of Baconburg were prone to spying on one another. But new-to-town pretty ladies and widowers whom everyone thought should have started dating again made for pretty interesting viewing, especially in late summer when there was nothing good on TV.

He took a breath to holler out a hello when his gaze fell on his cowboy hat. He couldn't count the times he debated if it was time to put the hat away for good but something always stopped him.

His stomach coiled like a fist twisting in his gut. He stared at it for a moment. Another deep breath. "Miss

Bennett? I just brought over the things on your list. I'm going to leave them on the kitchen table, if that's…"

The kitchen door swung inward and there stood Polly.

"…okay with you," he finished quietly as he settled the bag on the old oak table without taking his eyes off her once.

Her hair looked as if she'd just stepped out of a whirlwind, and her cheeks were pink. She was barefoot, had a muddy paw print on her neck, dirt on her nose and was wearing a big black garbage sack as a kind of poncho that didn't quite hide her rolled-up pink sweatpants and tie-dyed T-shirt.

Sam wouldn't have been more impressed, or surprised, if she had walked into the room in a sparkling ball gown. He grinned. He hadn't wanted to grin, or intended to grin, but one look at her and his mouth just sort of had a mind of its own.

"Sorry it took so long." She patted a wild strand of her hair down against her forehead, then heaved a sigh and sent that same wayward lock sailing upward again. "I've been wrestling with the native wildlife."

"Lucky wildlife." Yes, his mouth most definitely had a mind of its own around Polly Bennett. He cleared his throat. "I mean, I hope you won."

"Not yet I haven't. I did manage to get Homer in the bathroom, though." She went over to the sack he had just set down and began rummaging around. "I'm calling the little dog Homer for now because everything needs a name, don't you think? Anyway, then your brother called—"

"My brother? Max? Called you?"

"Yeah." She gave a nod, then turned and motioned for Sam to follow her. She hit the swinging door with her hip and paused long enough for him to shuffle by her, not seeming one bit slowed by his hesitant confusion. "Got my cell number from the principal, which in Atlanta would have made me uncomfortable, but here? That's like half a dozen kinds of small-town fabulous in a bucket, don't you think?"

"I might have to see that bucket first," he muttered as she hustled around in front of him and headed down a dimly lit hallway.

"Anyway, like I was saying, I had just wrangled him into the tub when your brother called." She opened the door to a small bathroom.

There in a big claw-foot bathtub sat the saddest-eyed, soaking-wet little puppy Sam had ever seen. It peered over the tub's edge at him and whined softly.

"Ta-da!" Polly threw her arms open wide in a triumphant flourish. "He's all yours."

"Ta-what?" Sam frowned, trying to make sense of things, a task made more difficult with Polly standing so near beaming up at him. "He's all…mine?"

"Not to keep. To bathe. Or help bathe. Max said you'd be happy to help." She had to squeeze to one side to get herself fully into the small, tiled room. "Said you knew all about this kind of thing."

"*What* kind of thing?"

She turned and cocked her head at him as if he was silly to have to ask. "Flea baths."

"Well, I…" How could he claim otherwise? He'd grown up on a farm, after all. He did know about tending to animals of all sorts. "Look, I just came over to drop off those things. Whatever Max promised, he did it without my knowledge or—"

"Please help me," she said softly. "I've never had a dog and I'm scared I'll get soap in his eyes or the special shampoo will burn and he'll think I'm being mean to him and not trust me anymore."

"—approval," he concluded, because he was the kind of man who followed through on what he started, even if it was concluding that he wasn't going to start anything.

"Please, Sam." Her voice caught in her throat.

She paused to compose herself and he couldn't help noticing the tremble of her lower lip, the white-knuckled grip on the shampoo bottle and the threat of tears in those big eyes. He warned himself to resist the urge to rush to Polly's rescue. What good could come of it after all?

"He's kinda my only pal in town right now." Polly glanced over her shoulder at the dog, then turned and tipped her face up to settle her gaze directly in his. "Other than, well, *you*. I really don't want him to turn on me."

He looked into Polly's eyes. She and her puppy needed him. Sam simply could not say no. He pushed up his shirtsleeves and headed into the small space, chiding himself under his breath as he did, "So much for no complications."

Polly shut the door behind her in the tiny white-and-yellow bathroom and became instantly aware of how much of the small space was suddenly taken up by broad, masculine shoulders, long legs and cowboy boots.

Sam didn't seem to notice. He simply squatted down by the tub and ran his hand down the wriggling puppy's back. "You didn't use hot water for the little guy, did you?"

"No, of course not. I just had an idea. Would you excuse me a second?"

Polly slipped out the door, and when it closed, she hurried off to the kitchen where she snatched up the hat she had run over and still hoped to make right. As she turned, her plastic makeshift apron crinkled and she thought to grab another trash bag for Sam, to protect him from any splashes or shaking by the dog. Her bare feet pounded down the hallway. Just outside the room she took a deep breath, then eased open the door, pausing when she heard Sam speaking in a quietly compelling tone.

"Look, it's nothing personal, little guy. If it were just me I'd offer to have you live on our farm, but I have these three girls, you see, and they already are crazy about another dog, a dog you could never be, a dog their mom told them about."

Polly sank her teeth into her lower lip to hold back a tiny gasp of surprise at that news. Her gaze dropped down to the hat and she stroked it once, feeling all the worse at this glimpse into how staunchly Sam protected the things that still connected his family to his late wife.

"It's just that my girls need to move forward. It's not good to have someone like you around…to fall in love with…to remind me that there are some things you can't hold on to… I mean to remind them." He cleared his throat.

So now Polly knew. It wasn't his girls he was protecting but his own heart with those hard-and-fast rules. She drew in a deep breath and rapped her knuckles on the door. "Hey, back with your hat and a little something to help you keep…dry."

"Too late!" He looked up at her from where he sat, cross-legged on the shaggy pink bathroom throw rug, with the little dog in a sopping-wet towel in his lap. The animal lifted his head to nuzzle against the man's soaked shoulder.

The sight didn't just melt her heart; it made her knees weak and her chin quiver. She slipped inside the room, shut the door and sank to the floor beside the pair. "Aw. I missed it."

"Just round one." Sam held up one finger and the puppy licked it. Sam laughed. He twisted around and pulled the plug from the drain and the water began to swirl away. "The mixture has to set on him for two minutes, then a really thorough rinse."

Two minutes to sit here and watch Sam coddle her sweet canine charge. Two minutes so close to the man she could see his chest rise and fall slowly with each intake of moist, steamy air. Two minutes before they finished up, he walked away and Polly would have to honor his rules and honor her own commitment to do what was right for the girls, find her lost friend a home.

"So, what's his name?" Polly's plastic covering crinkled as she settled on the floor on her knees and stroked the dog's head.

"You're the one calling him—"

"The dog your late wife told the triplets about," she said softly. "I only ask because, well, I heard you talking to him about it and I thought, well, because I have this dog for now and Caroline will be in my class…"

"Donut."

The dog looked up when Sam spoke.

Polly understood the response as the man's quiet intensity made her unable to look away as well.

"Marie came up with these stories, see, after she got the news that her illness was terminal." Despite the warm, damp air around them, Sam's coloring grew pale. He kept his gaze cast downward. "This mixed-breed dog, called Donut, causes havoc for three little girls on a ranch and their dad, who was a cowboy."

"Ah." She reached for the hat she'd brought with her, but he began talking again before she could produce it.

"In the first story, they learn a lesson about the power of love and God's forgiveness. She didn't have time to write a second one." His jaw went tight. "It was Marie's way of leaving a little bit of herself behind for the girls. They have every word memorized."

"She must have been an incredible mom," Polly said in hushed awe.

Sam jerked his head up and at last their eyes met. He studied her, his mouth set in a grim line for a moment before the tension in his face eased and he nodded. "Yeah, she was. Thank you for saying so."

One last gurgle from the tub, a glug, then all went silent.

"Anyway, the triplets all agree this—" he pointed to the dog, who had almost fallen asleep in his lap "—is what the dog looks like."

If two minutes was all God granted her, then she would be grateful. Wasn't that the very lesson she had come to Baconburg to learn? That life was about enjoying what you had while you had it, not always chasing after something better, something more?

"A cowboy, huh?" She shifted her weight and became aware of the hat on the floor beside her. "That reminds me. Let's wash the tub out with really hot water, get some really good steam going and…voilà!"

She produced the hat.

"Voilà?" He squinted at the object in her hands with the hint of a smile playing over his lips. "Pretty fancy word for a doggy chew toy, don't you think?"

"It's not that bad." She brushed her thumbs along a rough patch in the felt. "It just needs a little TLC. Like someone else I know."

"You talking about me?" He pointed to his chest, his tone teasing.

The tension in the small space eased and she gave Sam a sidelong glance, a you-know-better tsk and a shake of her head before she leaned toward the dog she had been calling Homer. "I'm talking about him."

Homer lurched forward.

Polly took a cold, wet nose to the cheek and squealed in a mix of surprise and delight.

Sam burst out laughing. "Looks like he thinks *you're* the one who needs the tender loving care."

"Smart doggy." Polly laughed and swiped a wrist over her nose. When she looked up, she found two pairs of soft brown eyes studying her.

Warmth rose in her cheeks. She'd have blamed the hot water from cleaning the tub, but she hadn't started it yet. She scrambled to reach the faucets and turned the hot water on full blast. "I say we stuff the crown of the hat with a small towel and shape the brim a little like so, apply a little heat…" She held it over the cloud of steam and it went limp as a noodle.

She glanced back over her shoulder at Sam, wondering how to apologize for actually making things worse.

Only, Sam didn't look as if he expected an apology. In fact, he seemed to have completely moved on from the whole hat debacle and was getting the dog ready for that final rinse.

Something about his reaction didn't sit right with Polly, but she honestly couldn't say if it was because she distrusted the ease with which he dismissed the keepsake or because he didn't seem to notice how helpful she was trying to be. Was it so wrong that she wanted Sam to notice her in this one slice of time they would probably have together?

For all her big talk about not rushing or pushing or competing, Polly just couldn't let that slide. "You know, you look good in this hat. I'd be glad to replace it if you—"

"Not necessary." He ran his hand along the dog's back and peered into his fur. "The boots I need because I do pitch in around the farm, but the hat?"

"Maybe something else? Something that suits you? Let's see…" She pretended to analyze him, savoring every last moment of their time together. "A gray fedora?"

He frowned and shook his head.

"No. How about a white ship captain's hat?"

"If she tries to order me one of those, you have my permission to drag her keyboard into the yard and bury it," he instructed the yawning dog.

Polly giggled, then gave him one last look and confessed, honestly, "I think you'd look great in a brown trilby. You know, kind of like those dads on old black-and-white TV shows who came home from work to the house with the white picket fence?"

As soon as she'd said it, she wished she'd kept her thoughts, and her visions of Sam as the kind of man she hoped to one day have in her own life, to herself. "I'm sorry, that sounded silly, I know."

"Naw. I...I kinda like that image. All-American small-town dad. There are worse things people could see me as, I'm sure." He grinned, just a fleeting one, then ruffled the dog's fur and cleared his throat. "There is supposed to be a fine-tooth comb to get the fleas out of his coat. Would you go see if it's in the bag I brought?"

"Um, oh, sure." She jumped at the chance to put some space between them. It was time to get her priorities in order. She and Sam were a no-go. And if she hoped to make a home here in Baconburg, the sooner she accepted that and, as Sam had put it, "moved on"—

The chime of the doorbell cut through her thoughts and startled her. She glanced toward the bathroom, then the kitchen where she'd been headed, and decided to get the door, explain the situation if needed and then get back to her mission.

"Hey there, neighbor!" A perky woman with chestnut-colored hair in a long bob stood on Polly's doorstep holding a plate of brownies, which she thrust over the threshold about two beats before she surged into the house herself. The woman didn't even seem to take a breath as she launched into her one-sided conversation, looking around the place and edging farther inside all the while. "I'm Deb Martin. I live across the way. Hope you like sweets. I bake a lot. Sorry to just drop in like this. Hope it's not a bad…time?"

Sam strode out from the darkened hallway, tugging at the huge wet spot on his blue shirt.

"Well, well, well, Sam Goodacre." The woman crossed her arms and gave him a sly smile. "I thought I saw your minivan out on the street."

"He was just helping me give a flea bath to a little dog I found." Polly's words rushed out so fast that they all but tumbled over each other. "I don't want you to get the wrong idea."

"Wrong idea?" She pinched the plastic trash bag over Polly's grubby clothes and gave it a waggle that all but said it was clear they weren't up to anything too wild. "That Sam is finally associating with a girl besides his sister and children again? Nothing wrong with that in my book."

"It's not like that," Polly hurried to say. "We're just…"

"Friends," Sam supplied. "I'm just here helping out a friend, Deb."

"Yeah, I heard. Washing a dog." She made a show of tapping her chin with one finger as though thinking it over. "You know, you and I have been friends since high school, Sam, and I don't think you ever…"

"It'll never happen again." Polly rushed forward so fast that she nearly spilled brownies everywhere. From the cheerful teasing of Deb's tone, Polly truly believed she was just having fun...and maybe indulging in a little of the already-deemed-pointless matchmaking Sam abhorred.

But Polly couldn't get the quiet intensity of Sam's words to the little dog out of her mind. She understood what was beneath the rules. A man with a broken heart who feared if he ever stopped moving forward, his loss would be his undoing. Polly got that. She had long suspected her own family's drive had been more about working through the pain of their broken home than about money or accomplishment.

"Look, I haven't had to think about the rewards and drawbacks of Baconburg's small-town life since... well, never, really, because I was really young when we moved away from here, but I get it." Polly went to the front door and held it open. "I have to be above even the suggestion of impropriety. Sam, I appreciate your help, but I can take it from here. Deb, thank you for the brownies. I have a dog to rinse off and some flyers to make."

"That—" she told the little dog as she toweled him off in the closed bathroom after Deb and Sam had gone on their way "—is that. Why be in a hurry to find a guy? I have my hands full with you. Sam Goodacre? Well, he has his rules and his reasons and I have plenty of time to follow my dreams, right?"

The dog sneezed.

"Yeah, I know. I didn't completely buy it, either." Polly sank against the side of the tub and tried not to think of Sam coming through the front door of her little house wearing that brown trilby and a grin as he announced to her and the girls, "Honey, I'm home!"

Chapter Six

"He's just so sweet and happy. Looking at him just lifts my heart." The very next day Polly juggled her cell phone and adjusted the stack of papers clutched under her arm to walk down the sidewalk of the historic section of Baconburg, hoping to find more places that would post the lost-dog flyers. She glanced down at the golden-brown dog trotting along on a leash at her side and smiled. "I honestly don't know how I am going to deal with not seeing him every day but that's probably what needs to happen. It's a small town, so I'm told it will be nearly impossible, but I'm going to have to find a way to avoid him."

"I can't believe it. One day in good ol' Baconburg and you meet a great guy with all this baggage attached."

Polly certainly did not think of Sam's family or the issues they had with the dog as "baggage," but before she could set her sister straight on that, she needed to make one thing clear. "I was talking about Barkley, the little dog I found."

"I know you were and *I* was talking about the great

big man you found." Essie's voice was soft and teasing. She absolutely knew how to push all of her twin's buttons. "Oh, and I thought you were calling him Homer."

"Now that he's all cleaned up, he doesn't look like a Homer anymore. I'm trying out some new names." Polly paused to study the little fellow, who also stopped, circled around and then plunked his behind down on the sidewalk washed with late-summer afternoon sun. "Not that I have any say over it or that I can let myself get too attached."

"To the dog or to the—"

"To the dog," Polly over-enunciated each word before Essie could even suggest that Polly would allow herself to get too attached to a certain single-father pharmacist and former hat owner. Feeling quite pleased with herself for getting everything under control so neatly, she squared her shoulders, took a good breath and opened her mouth to continue.

Bam. Bam. Bam.

Polly gasped at the three quick raps on the glass behind her. She whipped her head around.

"What was *that?* What's going on?" Essie asked. "Are you okay?"

Polly's tensed shoulders eased and she couldn't help but smile at the familiar face looking out at her from the huge window of Downtown Drug.

"I'm fine. I'm just…" She paused to give Sam Goodacre a wave, then raised the flyers as if to ask if she could post one in his store. She might be able to avoid the puppy and its new owner in the future, but she was just going to have to get used to seeing Sam around. "I like to think of myself as embracing the realities of small-town life."

"What does that mean?" Essie asked.

Sam gave her a nod, pointed toward the front door of the store and started that way.

Polly gave the dog's leash a tug, not unlike what Sam's smile had done to her heart, she thought as she told her sister, "It means I have to call you back later."

"But I thought we were going to talk about my coming for a visit," Essie barged on, never one to be dismissed.

"Give me a chance to get settled." Polly reveled in the chance to be the bossier sister for a chance. Her heels clicked over the sidewalk at a happy, brisk pace. "We'll talk later."

"Later when?" Essie sounded snappish, but Polly heard the concern in her twin's voice. "I need to know so I can make plans, Polly. You know how busy I am. How long will it be before I can come to see you?"

"How long? Why, as long as it takes. And not a minute more, I promise." Polly clicked off the phone and slid it into her pocket. When Sam didn't meet her at the door, she stretched her neck to peer back into the window again only to find an elderly couple had sidetracked him. The older man kept gesturing with a bottle of some kind of pills while the woman, her reading glasses perched on the end of her nose, kept trying to read the label.

"I think Sam might be a while," she told the dog. "So do we wait?"

A kid whizzed past on a bicycle so close and so fast that it set the papers under her arm flapping. Polly *could* hang around under the guise that she needed to ask Sam if he would post her flyer in his window.

"Or I could move on. I still have lots of flyers to distribute," she told the dog.

Barkley, or Homer, or whatever name he'd end up with, gave his head a shake that sent his ears slapping against his head. The leash jangled where it attached to his collar. He sneezed, then looked up at Polly, his tail wagging.

She started to lean down to murmur, "Bless you," when the front door came swinging open.

"Hi, Miss Bennett. How are you?" A small redhead in a pink top with a ruffled collar came bounding out into the entryway of the store. "Dad says you have posters for your lost dog. If you want, I can take them *all* and hand them out for you."

The way she stretched out the word *all* put the teacher on high alert. Polly had dealt with small children with their own big agendas before, so she wasn't ready to oblige that quickly. "That's a sweet offer, Juliette, but the dog and finding his owners is my responsibility."

"I'm not Juliette. I'm Caroline." The girl rose up on the ball of one foot and did a spin.

"That might work on other people, but you and your sisters are not going to be able to fool me that easily." Polly smiled. "Now, if you want to take one poster to put up in your dad's—"

"Deal!" Juliette snagged the page that Polly offered, turned around and ran back to the front door. As she swung it open she looked back and said, "Thanks,

Miss Bennett. I'll send Hayley and Caroline out to get posters, too."

Before Polly could call out to tell the child that the goal was to get as many flyers out to different people who might actually help find the owners as possible, Juliette disappeared inside the store. Polly sighed, stole a look in the big window to spot Sam moving his finger as if emphasizing the small print on the large pill bottle to the couple, who were crowded in close to him. For all his talk about moving on, he sure knew how to take his time and take care of others, didn't he?

"Miss Bennett!" A child in a green-and-white T-shirt came rocketing out the door so fast that she set the dog next to Polly woofing in surprise. "Hi, Donut!"

"Actually, I'm calling him…" Polly caught herself before she said anything that might lead the child to think Polly had even considered keeping the animal. "I'm sure whoever his real owners are have given him a perfectly good name. Let's not create any confusion by calling him Donut, okay, Hayley?"

That was not a phony excuse. Allowing the triplets to name the little dog that everyone agreed resembled the character in their mother's stories might well lead to emotional attachments and confusion, not to mention greater hurt when the little guy went back to the home where he truly belonged.

"But he *looks* like Donut," Hayley insisted. "Oh, and I'm not Hayley. I'm Caroline. You know, the one who is going to be in your class this year?"

"Oh, I *know* the Caroline who is going to be in my class this year. And you're not her." She handed the girl one of the flyers as if it were a lovely parting gift for having played the game, then gave her a pat on the back. "Nice try, though."

This time the child returned to the store with a bit of an obstinate stomp in her step. Just before she went over the threshold she gave Polly a narrowed-eyed glare. "Are you sure I'm not Caroline or are you just guessing to make us think you can tell us apart?"

"I can *really* tell you apart," Polly assured her.

"Hmm." And Hayley was gone.

Polly stood there for a moment not sure if she should go inside and tell Sam what the girls were up to or just move on with the task at hand. On one hand he might appreciate knowing, but on the other they were just testing boundaries and it wasn't anything she and Essie hadn't tried at that age.

The drugstore door swung open a third time. For one second, two, three, nobody came out. Then slowly, with two other sets of hands pushing her shoulders and hips, a redheaded girl in a strikingly familiar pink shirt with a ruffle at the neck, reluctantly appeared.

"Hello...Miss Bennett. Caroline asked me, Juliette, to come out and get a flyer for her like the one you gave me, Juliette, the ballerina." The girl lifted her arm in an arc, halting but in pretty fair ballet form.

"Okay, but I don't want to waste any of these. Promise you'll try to share this with someone who can help get this poor lost doggy home again, okay...*Juliette?*"

She nodded without making eye contact, snatched the paper away, then moved back to the still-open door.

'Fess up. Polly willed Caroline to come clean and admit who she was and what she had been put up to.

For a moment Polly felt herself in Caroline's place.

Always the sister in the shadow. She knew that struggle between wanting so badly to be like her more outgoing sister and wanting to just be herself.

Caroline hesitated outside the doorway. Her head bowed slightly, she stole a backward glance. Her gaze fell to the dog.

Honesty is the best policy. I know that's who you are, Polly wanted to urge the child. But she wasn't going to push or make a scene. If she just waited, Polly felt certain the girl would do the right thing on her own, in her own time.

The child sighed and then raised her gaze to Polly, her expression open and vulnerable. "Oh, Miss Bennett, I'm not Juliette. I'm Caroline."

Polly's heart soared at the child's decision to confess. "I know. I knew all along."

"She knew. She knew all along," Caroline said into the open door.

Suddenly two sets of hands yanked the girl back inside.

Polly rolled her eyes, laughed, then tugged on the leash to get her companion up and moving again. "I think maybe it'll be better if we walk back down to the corner, cross over and see if we can put up flyers in the stores across the street."

They had hardly taken two steps when the door to Downtown Drug swung open again.

"Whatever you've cooked up, you'd better understand right now I am not falling for..." Polly's shoulders went back in her best full-on teacher-about-to-lay-down-the-rules mode. Her shoes squeaked qui-

"I know. You have your rules," she murmured softly. Her words confirmed that she understood, but her eyes told a different story.

Or maybe that was Sam just wishing he had seen disappointment where there was actually relief that he ~~didn't~~ ~~let the moment~~ get the better of him. It would

etly as she turned slowly to confront…Sam Goodacre. "You."

"I'll take that under advisement," he said softly.

She had just told Sam she wasn't falling for him. She hadn't meant it as a proclamation, but now that it was out there, Polly sort of wanted to take it back. "I was just… Your girls were trying to…"

He held his hand up. "I know. Or rather, the minute I saw Juliette and Hayley making Caroline trade shirts with Juliette I knew what they were up to. Sorry they pulled a fast one on you."

"They didn't pull anything on me." She smiled and wriggled her fingers at him to wave goodbye before she pivoted and began walking again. "I knew which one was which from the start."

"You did?"

"Yep." She heard his footsteps hurrying behind her but she didn't look back. She just kept walking with a spring in her step, not unhappy to have him following along. "And don't be too hard on them. Juliette wasn't really trying very hard to fool me and when I told Hayley I could tell them apart, I think she took that as a challenge."

"Sounds like her." And just like that, he was walking alongside her.

Following was one thing, even calling out to her, but walking through town with her? "Aren't you supposed to be working?"

"I think it will be okay." He grinned at her and sidestepped the dog's meandering gait. "I know the boss."

She had to hurry to keep up with his long, determined strides, and the dog, seeming to pick up on

Sam's energy, rushed ahead, yanking Polly's arm out in front of her. How had her leisurely stroll through the old part of town become a mad dash? At least she had already made stops at the stores they passed along the way.

"Look, I don't want to pressure you or anything." A car passed by and the driver tooted a quick honk. Sam waved.

"Pressure?" Polly waved, too, even though she had no way of knowing who it was. It just seemed the neighborly thing to do even as she rushed along trying to figure out what pressure Sam was about to put on her.

They reached the corner and Sam turned to look down at her. "I just wanted to ask you how the search for the dog's owners is coming."

"Oh." The light turned red. Polly hoped her face was not as bright a shade. "Yeah, um, Barkley."

"What?"

"I started calling him Barkley."

"You're keeping him, then?" Sam's mouth had a serious set that had not been there moments ago.

"No, I'm not. I'd like to...*like* to? I'd love to." She looked down at the dog, who gazed up at her with those sweet brown eyes.

The light turned green. The dog jerked on the leash. For a split second Polly didn't know whether to go or stay. Finally she took a deep breath and stepped off the curb. "But I can't. It's not right."

"Because he doesn't belong to you?"

"Because it wouldn't be fair to you," she shot back over her shoulder.

"Me?" He hurried into the street after her, her arm and spun her around to face him. "W you talking about?"

"You're the one who told me about the realities o. small-town life, how paths cross and you see each other everywhere. And you're the one who doesn't think the girls are ready to deal with a dog so similar to Donut. So it just seems like I need to respect that and not keep the dog, especially because I'll be teaching Caroline and seeing her every day, probably telling the class about what the dog and I are doing…"

"You're giving up the dog for the sake of my girls?"

She nodded.

"Polly…I…" He stared into her eyes.

A car honked.

Polly jumped and started to scurry across toward the other side of the road.

Sam, his hand still cradling her elbow, headed back the way they came. They ended up doing a spin right there in the intersection. At least it gave the driver the opportunity to swerve around them.

"Just kiss her and stop holding up traffic," the man called as he whisked by. "What are you waiting for?"

"Kiss her? I hardly know…" Sam's gaze swung from the moving vehicle to the face of Polly Bennett and in that instant all the intensity of his denial evaporated. Another place, another time, another intersection, even, and he might have just thrown away all his reservations and swept this pretty little schoolteacher up in an impulsive kiss. "I didn't mean that as a slight. It's just that…"

didn't let the mom~~e~~ have made quite a story to live down, after all. New teacher steals smooch with local single dad!

He and Polly might as well have taken a billboard out proclaiming their mutual attraction. As it was, Sam still had time to save this mess. He backed away from Polly, stepping carefully over the leash to do so. With his smile fixed, he jogged back to the corner of the street while Polly tugged the puppy along, letting it stop and sniff around along the way. Finally they all hopped up onto the curb on the opposite sides of the street. Now, there was the perfect metaphor for the two of them, he thought. Two people heading toward their own goals, moving at their own pace, too much between them to really ever move forward together.

He looked at her, fussing to untangle herself from the dog's leash. The more she chased after it, the more the dog wound himself around her. Polly Bennett. She was enough to make a guy rethink his whole reasons for his unbreakable set of rules.

She jerked her head up and looked right at him, then lifted her shoulders and laughed at her predicament.

Sam raised his hand to say thanks and…

"Hey, Dad! Uncle Max says to invite Miss Bennett to dinner tonight," three little voices all hollered in unison as they ran full blast down the sidewalk toward him. But when they reached the corner, they all turned and put every last ounce of their considerable energy into making Polly hear the message. "Uncle Max says you have to come out to our house tonight. He's gonna *cook!*"

Sam held up both hands, thinking to tell his girls to take it down a notch, and realized too late it looked as if he might just be surrendering to them. He turned to Polly and shouted, "I understand if you don't—"

"I'd love to say yes, but—" Polly called out at the same time.

She'd love to say yes. To come to his home. Sam glanced over his shoulder at his girls.

"I wouldn't feel right leaving the dog home alone." Polly gave the leash a waggle and the puppy did an excited dance at seeing the girls.

"Bring him with you," the trio squealed in delight at Polly. Followed by three bright, expectant faces focusing on Sam and asking, "Why not?"

Polly in his home. With his girls. And that dog. It was everything that he had been trying to keep from happening. But when all those sets of eyes fixed on him that bright summer day, what could he do?

He was the guy who always moved forward, after all. And having Polly get to know the girls so she could help him guide Caroline wasn't exactly a detriment. Sam sighed and threw his hands up, this time in actual surrender.

"Why not?" He turned toward Polly and shook his head. "We close the store at five-thirty, and dinner is served about an hour after that. We'd love to have you."

Chapter Seven

Polly rang the doorbell of the large white-frame farmhouse shortly after six. Then, feeling anxious about the dog and the girls and the man she thought might answer the door any second now, she glanced around. Muffled footsteps thundered toward her from behind the door. Since it was too late to run, she bent, scooped up the dog and clutched him close and whispered, "It's you and me, pal. Us against Sam's rules."

The dog squirmed but didn't try to get down.

Hayley swung the door open wide. "Hey, Miss B!"

Juliette extended her arm toward the entryway and made a bow. "Please come in."

Caroline peeked around the door, ending up nose to cold nose with a certain brown-eyed mutt. "Hi, Donut!"

Polly managed a nervous smile and crossed the threshold. A savory aroma drifted into the foyer from the direction of a well-lit doorway to a room clearly filled with laughter and the clatter of dishes. She surveyed the distressed wooden floors, the walls painted in historic hues of sunny-yellow and French-cottage-blue, like something from a magazine. Or a storybook. Or a dream.

The Goodacre girls pressed in close to pet the pup and vie for Polly's attention. They made Polly's heart light.

"Hey, girls, at least let Miss Bennett get inside the house before you swarm all over her." Sam came striding down the hall in jeans, a plaid shirt, untucked, his hair damp as if he'd just cleaned up, wearing socks and with his boots in hand.

Kids. Dog. Laughter. Kitchen. Family. Home. Sam. This wasn't just any dream. This was Polly's dream, come true.

If for only the next few hours.

"Hi." Sam reached her side and settled his empty boots on the floor just inside the doorway.

"Hi." It wasn't exactly sizzling conversation.

The girls giggled.

Polly felt self-conscious. Then she remembered the hostess gift she'd tucked in her bag. "Oh, I brought something for you all. Actual tupelo honey brought with me from the South."

She shifted the dog in her arms to try to get to the heavy mason jar of the rich, sweet honey. The girls all stuck their hands up to try to help her.

Sam stepped in. "If it were winter, I guess I'd offer to take your coat, but seeing as it's not…may I take your dog?"

Polly laughed and handed off the little guy into Sam's strong, welcoming arms. The dog promptly slurped Sam's face.

The girls exploded in another round of giggles.

Polly pressed her lips together to keep from joining them, uncertain if Sam would be irritated, what with his whole no-dog rule and all.

Sam burst out laughing.

The very air around them seemed to ease. Sam set the dog down in the kitchen and directed the girls to set up a bowl of water. Each one wanted to be the one to do it. Max called out a hello to Polly and splashed some olive oil into a pan of vegetables with such style that for a second Polly wondered if she should offer to introduce Sam's younger brother to her twin sister, the chef.

But before she could do that, Gina came up, wiping her hands on a tea towel and, stealing a peek down at the dog lapping at the water, asked, "So, no response yet?"

Yeah, my first response is that I want to move in here and stay for, oh, just the rest of my life, Polly thought. What she said, though, was, "Huh?"

"To your lost-dog flyers? No responses?"

"Oh, the dog!" Polly laughed under her breath at her own scattered thought process, and shook her head. She reached into her purse and produced the jar of honey and offered it to Gina. "Nope, not a single call."

Gina took the jar, said a soft thank-you and then showed it to Max.

"Deb Martin, who lives across the street from me, says she's never seen him around the neighborhood." Polly looked around the room to find Sam pulling out a chair at the table for her. She moved over and allowed him to scoot the seat in. His hand touched her shoulder as she did. A sweet shiver shimmied down her spine as she forced herself to stay relaxed and finish her thought. "No one seems to know where he came from or where he might belong."

All three little girls drew in a breath like a choir about to launch into a robust refrain.

Sam gave them a look.

Max slid the lid onto a pot bubbling on the stove and announced dinner would be served soon.

"I can't wait," Polly said. "I didn't realize you were both a carpenter and a chef."

"Max? He's a jack-of-all-trades, all right. And a first-class cook," Sam muttered, going to the sink to wash up after handling the dog and directing the girls to do the same as he singled out Polly's gaze in the bright, bustling setting. "If by first-class you mean he cooks like he's had only one lesson."

"Play nice." Gina gave Sam's shoulder a shove before joining Polly at the table. She rolled her eyes and shook her head. "Brothers! Do you have any?"

"One." Polly held up one finger, then started to hold up a second to add that she also had one sister but before she could get it out, the girls scrambled, each trying to get a seat beside her.

"Oh, now! All three of you can't sit next to Miss Bennett." Gina jumped up to try to separate the triplets from trying to crawl all over each other and into one of the chairs on either side of Polly.

"There's only room for two," Sam warned, pulling back the chair to Polly's left.

"And one of those two is me!" Max slipped deftly into the seat Sam had slid away from the table.

Sam glared at him, then glanced at Polly.

"I guess that means the other one has to be me." And just like that, Sam took the seat on the other side of Polly. "To keep her safe from you."

"Brothers!" Gina shook her head and everyone shared a laugh.

Dinner was a charming mix of chaos and calm. Pasta made from locally milled flour, eggs from their own chickens and a sauce brimming with Goodacre-grown tomatoes, zucchini, carrots and scallions in the mix. Gina pushed back from the table first, complimenting Max on the meal and accepting accolades for her contribution, a dessert of peach cobbler with homemade ice cream on top.

"It's still light out. Can we show Miss Bennett around the farm now, Daddy?" Hayley tossed her napkin onto the table, practically spilling out of her chair.

"Maybe your dad should do those honors. We have dishes to clean up." Gina stood, raising her own plate as an example of the work awaiting them.

"The farm is your baby, Gina. You've done so much with it in the last few years. You deserve to show it off." Sam leaned back and patted his flat stomach, stretched, then gathered his silverware onto his place. "We guys will take care of the dishes tonight."

"What guys? I cooked. Family rules for meals are 'He who cooks it, books it.'" Max jerked his thumb over his shoulder. He stood, too, empty-handed, and offered his arm to Polly. "My work is done here. I'd be happy to escort you around the old farmstead, Miss Bennett."

"First, that's not a family rule. That's a Max rule,"

Gina picked up Polly's plate and headed toward the sink. "And we all know…"

"Max doesn't follow the rules," Sam said in a low, rumbling voice, his gaze aimed at his brother.

"Why don't we all pitch in?" Polly pushed her chair back and stood, avoiding Max's still-offered arm as she reached over to pick up the nearly empty pasta platter on the table. "That way it will get done faster and we can all go take the tour of the farm."

"You don't have to do that." Sam reached for the platter. Their hands brushed and their gazes met in the warmth of the kitchen lit by the fading sun of late summer. "You're the guest."

"Yes, I'm the guest." On one hand she didn't like being reminded, but on the other, it was probably a good idea. "I believe one of the *real* family rules around here is that guests get to choose what we do. I choose to help out."

Faster than Polly could cross the kitchen floor, the girls hopped up and began carrying their own plates and silverware to the sink.

Gina turned on the water.

Sam helped the girls clear the table.

Max directed Polly to where she could find foil and plastic wrap and whatever they needed to pack up the leftovers. They worked with each other like a family.

And it struck her how unlike her own family they were. No racing to see who could finish first or who did the best.

Polly paused for a moment to watch them all and it warmed her heart. This was the kind of family she had always longed for, one that worked as a team, not in competition.

The girls did display a bit of one-upmanship when they started off on the short version of the grand tour a few minutes later.

Max had conceded that because he had already seen the farm, had work to do and didn't believe he'd get a minute of Polly's undivided attention, he would stay behind. And Gina decided she should hang around the house to keep the dog company, because they didn't want to risk a bad interaction with any farm animals. Also she wanted to finish up some laundry so that when they returned, the girls could then get their baths and get to bed on schedule.

Of course, Polly saw right through their excuses and half expected Sam to protest the obvious attempt at setting them up. That he didn't made Polly cherish this one special night all the more. She drank in the fresh country air and the quaint setting, enjoying it almost as much as the company. She could get used to this sense of peace and quiet.

She shouldn't. But she could.

That quiet was broken when Hayley wanted the group to go see the chicken she had raised from a hatched egg for 4-H. Juliette wanted to use the open space to show off what she had just learned in ballet class, something called an arabesque. Caroline quietly murmured to Polly that she had named each animal they owned.

"Isn't there a caution about not naming farm animals that might become meals?" Polly asked Sam out of earshot of the girls as they strolled through a wooden gate with the girls in the lead.

"We don't eat any of our livestock. We use them for eggs, milk and cheese," Sam explained. "No judgment on anyone who does. We all like a good burger here, after all."

Sam moved ahead of the group and swung open a door in the side of a red barn with white trim that looked like a painting from a child's picture book. "When we were kids, our folks used to raise hogs that ended up as ham and bacon. It's just not part of what Gina is doing now. Things change. Change is good. I think it's healthy, don't you?"

Polly moved ahead of him through the open door.

"Watch me! Watch me! Watch me!" Juliette bounded into the wide pathway between large stalls on either side of the barn.

Polly tried to follow the action but just as she did, another triplet started up.

"My chicken has its own special nest. Over here, Miss Bennett." Hayley leaped up and down, waving her hand. "Over here."

Caroline looked around, seeming even more lost and uncertain of her place in the large space with her sisters vying for the spotlight.

"Well, yes, change can be good." Polly's chest tightened. How did she get this father to see what she saw? To consider that what worked for him was right for his girls? Who was Polly to talk to him about that, anyway? She glanced over at Caroline gazing off into the rafters while the other girls hurried here and there. She was that sister who didn't quite fit in, that sometimes felt invisible to her parents, that's who. "And I'd never tell you that moving on with things is a bad idea—"

"Great, I'm glad you feel the way I do about it." Sam put his hand on Polly's back and propelled her forward. "That's going to make getting things going so much easier."

"Getting…what…" Polly tried to look back at him even as her feet obeyed his urging her onward.

Straight ahead, Juliette extended one leg out straight. Her knee locked, she raised it high behind her and bent forward. "See, Miss Bennett? My teacher says my arabesque is the best in my class."

Hayley ran for a large wire cage housing a fat black-and-white hen and started clucking at the bird. "This is my chicken. Also be careful where you walk because the barn cat is gonna have babies and she's around here somewhere."

"Daddy says we can't name the kittens, though, because those have to find new homes." Caroline seemed buffeted about in the shuffle of it all.

Polly knew just how that felt. She wanted to throw her hands up and ask everyone to just be still for a moment so she could think. Her head was virtually spinning.

Or maybe it wasn't virtual.

Juliette did a turn.

Hayley moved in a circle around her chicken's cage.

Sam snagged Polly by the elbow and turned her around to face him. "I need your help with Caroline."

In that moment, his humble request, the caring in his voice and the sincerity in his eyes quieted the chaos around them. If she had taken the time to let her heart say a prayer about the situation earlier, it would have been for this, for Sam to invite her into his life and the lives of his girls in just this way.

"We have got to get Caroline involved in some things apart from her sisters. That's where you come in."

Where she came in and where she wanted to get off the merry-go-round. She took a deep breath and reminded herself that if she had prayed for anything it should have been for how best to do God's will.

In the distance Gina's voice called out that it was time for the girls to come in and take their baths.

Sam motioned for the girls to do as their aunt asked.

"Walk us up to the house, Miss Bennett." Juliette and Hayley rushed up to Polly, each taking her hand and tugging her off to the door again.

Sam swept Caroline up easily in his strong arms and tagged along behind them.

"What were you and Miss Bennett talking about, Daddy?" Caroline asked loudly enough for Polly to hear although the other girls did not seem to notice.

"I was just letting her know that we have big plans for you this school year, sweetie. Right, Miss Bennett? You with me on that?"

With him? Polly's heart pounded. All she wanted to do was run away right now. She needed some perspective, which she couldn't get surrounded by these girls or that man carrying his daughter on the pathway of their sweet farm home.

She put up her hand. "This is something we should talk about later, don't you think?"

"I'll look forward to it," Sam said quietly but with a new energy in his step. Clearly the man thought he had formed an ally in pushing his child to fit the ideal he had formed for his family.

Polly's heart sank and when she saw her little lost dog bouncing down the porch steps at the sight of her, she couldn't help but wonder if he truly was her best and maybe only true friend in Baconburg.

Sam watched the girls make their way up the porch steps, each of them taking a moment to pet and coo over the animal Polly Bennett had brought with her for the evening. The dog lapped at their little hands, making them squeal with delight. Juliette tried to hug the dog around the neck. Hayley tried to pick him up around the middle. The excited pup whipped around and whapped Caroline in the legs with his tail. More squeals and laughter.

"Don't… He's too big for… Put the dog down…" Gina couldn't finish a thought, and she couldn't get her hands on any kids or the dog's collar. It was as if his sister didn't even know where to begin.

Polly did not have that problem. She dived in without hesitation and scooped up the dog in both arms, lifting him out of the girls' grasping fingers but still holding him so that they could stroke his paws and ears. It was the perfect solution.

Sam leaned back against the porch rail to savor the image for a moment. He'd had his reservations about Polly coming to his home, but when he couldn't avoid it, he didn't dwell on the problems it presented. He pressed on and made the best of the situation. Now he had Polly on his side.

He looked at her and their eyes met. Polly on his side? The implications of having this dark-haired woman with the enormous heart anywhere near him made him pause. It went against everything he had worked so hard to create for his girls—a safe situation where they could continue to grow without having to suffer more loss and disappointment.

Polly felt anything but safe to him.

"I guess this is my cue to thank you for a lovely meal and say it's time for me to head home." Polly stepped away from the girls.

The girls all groaned and followed after her.

"You don't have to go yet." Hayley thundered down the steps to put herself directly on the path in front of Polly.

"We'll take our bath really fast if you promise to read to us before bed." Juliette's feet barely hit the ground as she rushed up to Sam and spun around in front of him as if she expected him to back her up. "That's okay, right, Daddy?"

"It's okay with me…" Sam cringed at playing the big softy. Was he trying to pretend to himself that it was only the girls who wanted Polly to stay a little longer? "But Miss Bennett just said she needed to go."

"She didn't say *need*," Hayley corrected.

Sam drew a breath to launch into a lecture about not badgering their guest when Caroline moved around from behind Polly, looked up, and as she stroked the dog's muzzle, said quietly, "Oh, please, Miss Bennett, please stay long enough to read us a Donut story after our bath."

It was like a double sucker punch to the gut for Sam, hearing Caroline's earnest plea and yet not sure how he felt about Polly reading his late wife's story to his matchmaking daughters. "I don't think that's such a—"

"I printed out a few copies. Let me get you one," Gina, who had been waiting at the open door, volunteered.

"Girls, really?" Sam put his hands on Juliette's and Hayley's shoulders and urged them up the steps alongside him. "We invited Miss Bennett out for dinner, then let her help clean up, dragged her all over the farm and now we're trying to make her do bedtime-story-reading duty?"

"I hardly think of it as a duty," Polly said softly.

"But you're our guest." Sam reached her side.

"That's right, and company gets to pick." Hayley made a break and headed for the front door, swinging it open.

"You want to pick to read to us, right, Miss Bennett?" Caroline asked so softly that Sam wasn't quite sure he heard it or just imagined she'd expressed it with her eyes, so like her mother's, fixed in fascination on her new teacher's face.

Polly looked at him, silently asking for his approval or for him to make an excuse so she could back out without being the bad guy.

Sam smiled and shook his head. Never in his wildest dreams could he see Polly as the bad guy. The wrong girl, here at the wrong time, yes. But bad guy?

"I think Marie would have liked knowing Caroline's teacher would one day read the story she wrote to the girls."

Polly smiled a smile that Sam could not get out of his mind the whole twenty-five minutes it took for the girls to get quick baths, get into their pajamas and climb into bed.

Gina had done bath duty, then stayed to clean up the bathroom and get damp towels in the laundry.

Max stopped in to tell the girls good-night, then grumpily excused himself to his own room saying his "boss" expected him to be at work on the lunch-counter project bright and early.

Polly had taken that time to take the dog for a walk and read over the text of the book once, saying she wanted to do it justice.

Sam appreciated that on many levels. Still, when the time came for the big "performance," he just could not stand by and watch Polly with the girls reading aloud Marie's words. Words written so those girls would not forget their mom and the love she and God shared for them.

"'Three precious girls with blue eyes and red curls...'" Polly began to read from the pages that Gina had typed up and printed from the story Marie had written by hand a year before her death.

Sam turned away at the girls' room door.

"That's about us." The hushed excitement in Caroline's voice carried all the way into the hall.

Suddenly instead of hitting the stairs, heading for the front door, getting as far away as good manners would allow, Sam's footsteps slowed.

"I know it's about you three." Polly's tone was kind and warm. "In fact, looking at you all here now, it's like having your mom's book spring to life right in front of my eyes."

Sam had often felt that very thing, but hearing Polly discuss Marie so openly in front of the girls hit him hard. Then when he heard the familiar old creak of the rocking chair that Marie used to sit in to sing to the girls or comfort them in when they had a bad dream, the sound practically knocked the air right out of his lungs.

He spun around to rush back into the room, wanting to put a stop to it all, to spare his daughters the same angst that had his chest tight and his jaw clenched. "Maybe this isn't such a good—"

"We think about our mom whenever we say our prayers," Juliette said softly.

Sam froze just outside the door, looking in at the precious faces of his girls gazing adoringly up at Polly in the nearby rocking chair.

"Do you say prayers, Miss Bennett?" Hayley asked outright.

"Yes, I do. And I know that God hears them. Prayer is a powerful thing."

"Do you pray for something special, Miss Bennett?" Again it was fearless Hayley who forged ahead.

"Not *for* something, as in to *get* something, but…" Polly's expression grew slightly somber. "I pray for my students and the school and my family."

"And Donut," Caroline prodded.

Sam peered in to find three little girls sitting on one bed with a funny-looking, long-bodied dog stretched out across them all, managing to get some part of himself petted by each one of them. The contented animal struggled to keep his eyes open.

Polly reached out and stroked the dog's head. "And Donut."

"Don't you miss your family, Miss Bennett?" Hayley asked.

"Well, I haven't actually been away from them for very long, and I can talk to them whenever I want." Polly leaned back in the rocking chair.

"We miss our mom." Caroline's voice was strong but still.

"I am sure you do, but isn't it like a little visit from her whenever you hear the story she wrote for you?"

"It is, but we don't get to hear it very often," Juliette said.

"But you can hear it now," Polly assured them.

The papers rattled. The rocker creaked. Polly took a deep breath, then launched into the story about Donut, the dog who couldn't do anything right and only wanted to be loved. She did not miss a beat or stumble over a single syllable. She used her voice to convey every emotion and sentiment.

For the first time since he had heard the tale from Marie's lips, Sam found himself reminded of the message behind the story—that God meets us where we are and loves us even though we are not perfect.

Sam leaned back against the wall of the hallway outside the bedroom and waited as the story concluded and Polly said good-night to each of the girls.

He leaned into the doorway just as she finished up and promised the girls he'd be back to check in as soon as he saw Donut and Miss Bennett to her car. Donut—yes, even he couldn't fight the urge to call the little guy that—reluctantly but obediently clambered down from the bed and padded softly to the hallway.

One by one Juliette, then Hayley slid from Caroline's bed and got into their own. Polly rose from the rocker and wriggled her fingers to the girls as she told them good-night and thanked them for inviting her out, telling them it was the very best time she'd had since arriving in town. She slipped by Sam and into the hallway where she told Donut to go on downstairs because it was time for them to go.

Sam stretched his upper body, his hand braced against the doorframe, but he kept both feet outside the threshold. "Good night, girls. Thank you for being such good hostesses to Miss Bennett. Now say your prayers and go to sleep."

"But—" Hayley sat up on her bed with her legs crossed.

"Prayers, then sleep," he reiterated, cutting off any last-ditch efforts at matchmaking, at pleading for them to keep the dog. Well, at least for them to make those pitches to him. What they would pray about, he could just imagine, and thought it best not to hover with Polly so near to listen in on their requests. "I love you guys."

"We're not *guys,*" Juliette called back before all three sweet young voices joined to call out, "We love you, too, Daddy."

Sam started to pull the door shut but not before Caroline could add, "And Donut, too!"

Sam shut his eyes and pulled the door closed until it clicked. He took a deep breath, then turned around, took a step and almost tripped over his guest. He had to put his hands on her upper arms to keep from bumping into her.

"I hope I didn't overstep my bounds talking to the girls about their mom. I tried to be careful, but I also had to be honest." Polly did not flinch but held her ground, looking up at him with the most sincere eyes Sam had ever seen. "I wondered when they started asking questions if I should have followed your example and moved on without looking back right after dinner."

"I like having you here." He did not take his hands from her arms. Even though they stood in the open hallway, it felt as if the two of them were tucked away from everyone else in the world.

"It was a lovely dinner. I'm glad I came out to your family farm, too."

"I didn't mean the farm. I meant—" he searched her face, then leaned down, his face just above hers "—here."

"Oh." The single syllable made her lips so kissable.

And so he kissed her. Not a long or lingering kiss, but a sweet, stolen one, brief but still able to convey that he had wanted to kiss her from the first time he had come across her in the driveway.

She raised her hands and he half expected her to push him away, but instead she wound her fingers into the fabric of his shirtsleeves and that's where they remained even after the kiss ended and Sam stood there losing himself in her eyes.

"I guess I'm the one who should apologize for overstepping bounds now," he murmured.

Polly shook her head, her black hair swaying softly. "That would only apply if I had set up a boundary and you crossed it against my wishes."

"Well, a good host always tries to do as his guest wishes." He leaned in again and for an instant their gazes met. He looked deep into those kind, innocent eyes. He should pull back, turn and walk away. No good could come from this. There was no future here, regardless of what they wished.

Sam had learned the hard way in life that wishing was a waste of time. The only thing that helped was to keep moving in the right direction. Kissing Caroline's teacher was definitely the wrong direction.

And yet, he shut his eyes, leaned in and pressed his lips to hers again. For a second time there was nothing but the two of them, no past, no future, no rush.

Then the quietest gasp broke through to his conscious mind.

They jumped apart.

"Who was that?" Polly's head whipped around from the direction of the stairway to the dimly lit hallway lined by the family members' bedrooms.

Rustling came from behind the girls' door.

Down the hall, the door to Max's room rattled, then clicked shut.

From the stairway came Gina's way-too-obviously-loud "conversation" with Polly's canine houseguest. "Hey, little fella, where's the rest of the crew? They didn't send you down here all by yourself, did they?"

"It doesn't matter who it was—somebody saw what happened between us." Sam stepped back, his head bowed as he gathered his resolve.

"I know." Polly touched his arm, his cheek, then she, too, took a step back. "We have to make sure no one sees us doing that again."

"It's not that I wouldn't, under other circumstances, like to—"

"You don't have to explain. I'm Caroline's teacher. You have your rules. This is how it has to be." Polly held up her hand and retreated a step, still facing him. "School starts Monday. I won't have any reason to see you or the girls until…well, until Caroline gets to class then."

"Polly, if it were just me—"

"But it's not. It's the girls and your late wife and me and Donut, and…I get it, Sam. I don't like it, or maybe even agree with it, but I get it." She shook her head, then turned and hurried downstairs where Gina and the dog were waiting in the foyer.

And Sam let her go. As she has said, she was following the example he had touted time and again. No looking back. Keep moving forward.

He heard the front door shut. Then the car doors open and shut again. The engine started. The quiet little hybrid car chugged off. Not until the front door opened and shut again and he heard Gina moving around the first floor did Sam finally plod slowly down the steps. Knowing he would not see anything in the fading light but the empty drive leading to the country road, he stood at the door and gazed out the window that overlooked the porch. What he was looking for, he couldn't say. He only knew that he would never look around this place, the place where he had grown up and where he had retreated into the depths of his deepest pain, in the same way. After this evening, whenever he helped clean up the dishes or tucked his girls in he'd remember Polly there. And Donut, too.

And Sam wasn't sure he didn't kind of like the idea.

Chapter Eight

On the first day of school Polly woke up a full half hour before her alarm went off.

"Finally," she huffed, pushing off the covers and swinging her feet to the soft, braided throw rug by her bed. Glancing back over her shoulder at the sunrise just beginning to peek through a space between her closed drapes, she yawned and scrubbed her fingertips through her hair. "That was one of the longest weekends of my entire life!"

A soft snort from a certain golden-brown, adorable mutt seemed to challenge her.

"I guess that's one thing I didn't take into account when I moved to such a small town. Not a lot for a stranger to do besides work and go to church, especially if that stranger is an unmarried young lady trying to avoid that town's favorite single dad." She tried to keep it all light and cheerful, knowing she was only trying to convince herself of what she was pretending to tell her still-sleepy-eyed friend nestled in his doggy bed. "But I did get a lot more posters made to try to find you a home."

She made herself smile when she said that even though the very thought weighed heavy on her heart. After the visit from Deb Martin and still no calls about the lost pet, Polly had switched from looking for owners to looking for a forever home for the little guy.

She stretched and purposefully avoided looking at the new photo of the sweet dog's face above the caption I Could Be Yours.

"Did I say longest weekend of my life? I should have said the loneliest weekend of my life." She shut her eyes and willed herself not to go all misty-eyed over the thought of saying goodbye to what seemed to be her only connection in Baconburg. But after days of people telling her the Goodacre triplets were asking about the dog, Polly knew she couldn't keep the animal and keep her peace of mind. "I'm probably just missing my family, right?"

The truth was, she was missing a family that was not her own and never could be.

More than once on Saturday she had wondered what the Goodacre girls…and their dad…were up to. On Sunday morning she had tried to not get too distracted while looking around to see if they attended the small community church she had gone to at the invitation of a fellow teacher.

But today the week started all over and and the new school year would be under way. Polly couldn't wait to get into her classroom. She dressed and walked the dog and filled his water bowl and gathered her things and…dressed again. The outfit she'd planned out a week earlier suddenly seemed too young and fun. A week ago that might have seemed like a good idea, to project the image of an energetic teacher brimming with new ideas. But now?

"You never get a second chance to make a first impression." Polly muttered her mother's warning as she slipped into her navy blue pants and lavender shirt. But that's what she wanted to do, to make a new first impression on Sam Goodacre, and on his daughters, when they came in this morning escorting Caroline into her new classroom.

"Yes, I look like a no-nonsense professional educator," she told herself with one last glance in the rear-view mirror as she parked. "Not like a lost cause."

Thoughts of Sam, the triplets and the dog she was trying to place in a home of his own only added to Polly's already-churned-up emotional state. So when Brianna Bradley, one of the other two second-grade teachers, rapped on Polly's car window, Polly nearly jumped out of her skin.

"Hurry up!" Brianna motioned to Polly to get out of the car. "You're on parking-lot duty!"

"Parking...what?" Polly popped open the door and climbed out.

"I know, it's a rotten thing to do to the new teacher, but we're stuck until we get some parents to volunteer tonight." She pushed Polly toward the front of the school. "All you have to do is stand here and remind parents to keep moving thataway."

Brianna pointed toward the drive with Exit painted on it.

"But—"

"Go drop your things off in your room and flip

the light on. You can come inside five minutes before the bell rings. The hallway teachers will keep things in order until then." More pushing. "Say, do you still have that dog? I thought you'd have found a home for him before now."

"Um, yes, I…" She started to ask how Brianna knew about Donut, then glanced back to see the other teacher swiping dog hair off her sleeve where it had brushed against Polly's clothes. Polly looked down at the dark slacks in glaring daylight to see golden-brown hair clinging here and there. She sighed. So much for that first impression.

On the bright side, as parking-lot teacher she'd be so busy that if Sam brought the girls into their class-rooms, as many parents of young children did, she wouldn't have to interact with him. Confident in that, she began to try to brush away the worst of Donut's hair off her slacks.

Three quick honks startled her. She jerked her head up and jabbed her finger in the direction that Brianna had pointed earlier only to find Sam Goodacre smiling at her from behind the wheel of the family minivan.

"Miss Bennett! Miss Bennett! Will you be at Sign Up for Your School tonight?" Hayley Goodacre hadn't even gotten fully out onto the sidewalk before she started calling out.

Juliette and Caroline were not far behind.

"Hurry on into your classes, girls. You know the drill," Sam ordered through the lowered passenger-side window.

"You're not coming inside with them?" Polly shaded her eyes and leaned forward to peer in at him.

"Are you kidding? Treat them like 'baby' first graders? They'd never forgive me. They know what to do."

"Move forward." She nodded.

"It's not a bad thing, you know." He sounded defensive, as if what she thought of his parenting approach mattered to him.

She smiled at that idea, but couldn't allow herself to linger over the notion. "No, I mean, you're holding up the other parents dropping off kids." She waved him on. "Move forward."

"Oh, right!" He laughed and waved, rolled forward but slowed again long enough to say, "I'd like to see you tonight at the sign-up."

"Really?" Maybe it was the loneliness of the past weekend or nerves for the first day of school, but hearing Sam say he wanted to see her made her pulse quicken. Maybe the days since their kiss had him rethinking all his—

"We've got a lot to talk about to get Caroline started on the right track this year."

"Right. Caroline," she murmured under her breath. She pushed back her shoulders, raised her hand and gave another wave. "Move on, please."

This time she was sending a message to herself.

Sam had a plan. In his situation he couldn't afford not to. Although the past ten days—ever since he veered from his course to see if a certain young lady needed his help—Sam's plans hadn't seemed to mean a whole lot. But tonight, the first time the girls would be able to learn about and join school-sponsored clubs and learn about opportunities for after-school activities,

Sam had come up with something that couldn't fail. Divide and conquer. Three girls, three adults, one mission—to help Caroline plunge into at least one new adventure while keeping Hayley and Juliette from going off the deep end and signing up for a dozen each.

Sam had laid out the strategy carefully. Gina would guide Hayley through the crowd of colorful booths set up in the school gymnasium. Max would shepherd Juliette. And Sam would prod Caroline along as best he could. If any of them reached an impasse, they had agreed to go to the girl's teachers for advice.

Well, Max and Gina agreed. Sam felt confident *he* wasn't going to need any backup. Caroline was his daughter, after all. He'd just point out the advantages of the groups that he thought might help bring her out of her shell and that would be that.

"Caroline wants to join the book club." Sam poked his head into the open door of Polly Bennett's second-grade classroom barely five minutes after he had made that bold proclamation to himself.

"Good for her." Polly twisted around to look at him from her perch, standing halfway up a short stepladder, hanging scalloped trim along the top of a long bulletin board bearing the sign I CAN.

"Actually I was hoping you'd help her choose something else," Sam confessed, sheepishly. "I'd like her to be a Go-Getter."

"Joining the book club can be a way of being a—" Polly went up on her toes on the ladder rung, and stretched her whole body all the way to her fingertips to try to push in the last tack. The ladder wobbled.

In an instant Sam rushed to her side. Using his own

weight as ballast, he planted his boot on the bottom rung. While he grabbed the side of the ladder with one hand, the other cupped Polly's elbow to keep her steady. He leaned in to further protect her from falling, but at the last second she righted herself.

Looking down over her shoulder at him, a little breathless from the near spill, she finished her thought in a whisper. "A go-getter."

He should have pulled away immediately, especially after what had happened between them in the upstairs hallway at the farm. But standing there so close he could see the way her black bangs caught on the tips of her long eyelashes, the last thing on his mind was moving on.

"The Go-Getters is an after-school program to get kids involved in the community and keep them active." Reluctantly he took a step backward. "They go on supervised hikes, learn square dancing, do physical fitness challenges."

"Hiking and dancing? Sounds more like Juliette and Hayley's style." She stepped down a rung. The ladder rocked from side to side slightly.

"I know, but it's not like it's a bad thing for me to want that for Caroline, too, is it?" Sam held out his hand to help her down.

"Bad?" She slid her hand in his.

It felt good to be there with her, to stand so close to her, to be asking her advice about Caroline and trusting that what she said would bring with it the best of intentions.

Polly paused a moment gazing down at him. She shook her head just enough to make her hair sweep

free of her eyes as she pressed her lips together as if
maybe she was trying to keep herself from saying too
much. She took a breath, then stepped down to the
floor and tipped her head back to meet his gaze. "Not
for one moment do I think you want anything that
would be bad for Caroline."

"Thanks. I thought for a minute—"

"But…" She withdrew her hand from his.

He closed his suddenly empty fingers into a loose
fist and smiled, reminding himself of his conviction
that Polly had what was best for Caroline in mind. "But
what, Polly?"

"Sam, I just think you need to keep in mind that
your triplets might be identical, but they are still indi-
viduals. What works for one, or even two, might not
be right for the third sister."

"I've thought about that, Polly. I really have, but in
the car on the way here, we talked about doing things
that make us happy and Caroline told me she really
wanted to do that this year."

"Good, then I assume you've thought that maybe
she was saying that what she wanted to do this year
was make *you* happy."

Not since Marie had anyone spoken to him so directly and honestly about his handling of the girls. Sam
tightened his jaw. On one hand he liked finally hearing
somebody give him some real advice that might actually help him. On the other hand… "I think I know my
girls, Polly."

She nodded and moved to her desk.

Watching Polly sitting all proper in her teacher's
chair going over her day planner, he kept getting

flashes of her in his drugstore, her at his table. He could see Polly needing his help with her dog, Polly reading to his daughters. After this short time she was already that much a part of his life.

However, that didn't change the reality that she was a new girl in town who had told the triplets that she missed her family. What if she decided not to stay after the end of the school year? He couldn't risk what that might do…to his girls. No, better to stick with his plan, not because it was the best choice, but because for him, it was the only one.

He wanted to go over, put his hands on her shoulders and tell her that, but the sound of multiple little tennis shoe–clad feet came thumping and bumping down the school hallway outside the door.

"Daddy! Daddy! We all got signed up for clubs and stuff!" Hayley flapped a paper as she and Juliette practically tumbled over each other to get inside Polly's classroom.

"Hayley! Juliette! No running!" Gina's voice echoed after them followed by Caroline winding around into the threshold with a piece of paper of her own tucked tightly to her chest by her crossed arms.

"Hey, sweetie, did you join the book club?" Sam tried to sound enthusiastic. He really tried.

Caroline shook her head.

"The current-affairs club?" He went for the second choice on the child's list, more than a little surprised to find himself rooting for a positive answer.

Another shake "no."

"Then what did you join?" he asked, stealing a sideways glance at Polly.

"The Go-Getters!" Hayley and Juliette shouted in unison.

Caroline ventured forward, extending her hand to show him the paper he had to sign to allow her to join the club Sam had decided she should join.

He smiled, but deep down he couldn't help feeling a lump in the pit of his stomach. He looked down and shifted his feet, telling himself this was a good thing. Caroline needed this.

But when he raised his gaze to Polly's again, he couldn't help wondering if he had been fooling himself all along. Polly might just be right about the girls and it made his chest ache. How could he cope with knowing that the only person who could make him a better parent was the one person he believed also had the power to break his daughters' hearts?

Chapter Nine

"Friday at last!" Katie Williams, one of the other second-grade teachers, who was only a couple of years older than Polly, stuck her head in the open door Friday afternoon as the rest of the staff was heading home. "Big plans for the long weekend?"

"You mean they get *longer?*" Polly blinked at her teaching colleague.

"It's Labor Day, silly." Katie came in and leaned back against the wall, crossing her arms over her yellow-, red- and black-plaid apron bib dress. "We have three whole days off."

"Oh, that's right. I…uh…" Three whole days. It sounded like an eternity. It had her wondering if she was really cut out for small-town life. As soon as she thought that, memories washed over her to contradict it. From the first day when Sam lay on the drive to help her rescue the lost dog to the day his family invited her out to eat, she had loved every minute of that. Of course, that probably wasn't just small-town homeyness.

"I don't know. I've been so busy planning so that the school week stays on track I haven't put much thought into the weekends." Polly pulled out the large drawer of her desk where she kept her purse. Her gaze fell on her car keys and a sense of possibility seized her…or maybe it was panic. "I guess I could always go home to Atlanta to visit."

It was an impulsive idea, but once she'd said it, it didn't seem so far-fetched.

"Really? Atlanta?" Katie turned around to gaze at the map of the United States unrolled over the chalkboard from the last lesson of the day. She tipped her head and peered closer. "Isn't that, like, almost a twelve-hour drive?"

"Ten hours and about fourteen minutes, door to door," Polly murmured, thinking of how long it had taken to drive from her mother's home to her rented house in Baconburg. Then she drew in a deep breath and shook her head, losing enthusiasm for a weekend spent bouncing between her parents' respective houses and her sister's restaurant. The whole thing would be a blur. And she'd probably end up being reminded how much more her family expected of her. Could her self-esteem take it right now with her big, bold move for independence still so shaky? "Of course, that could be give or take fifteen minutes depending on *whose* door I chose to go to."

"So you'd spend most of tomorrow and then Monday in the car." Katie tapped her finger to her cheek and narrowed her eyes. "Not much time to visit. Then there's the issue of the dog… I guess you could take him with you."

And turn the way-too-happy-for-comfort puppy loose in her mom's perfectly appointed home or the home her dad now shared with the big, hissy cat given to him by his wife-to-be? Her sister's restaurant was obviously out and her brother was allergic. And really, deep down, Polly didn't want to go. "Maybe I'll just hang around Baconburg."

Katie perked up a little too much for such a non-committal remark. "So you're staying at home, then?"

At home. Polly liked that. She tugged her purse out of the drawer, grabbed her keys and tossed them up to catch them again. "Looks like that is exactly where I'll be."

"And you don't have plans?" Katie raised her voice.

"Nope, just to stay at home and—"

"Great!" Brianna Bradley popped into the room from the hallway where she'd clearly been hovering, waiting for this very news from Polly before she appeared. "That means you're available!"

"Available?" She pushed her chair back and stood up. "For what?"

"The Go-Getters are having an event tomorrow to raise money to go to the Museum Center in Cincinnati. It's a dog wash at the fire station."

Dog wash with the Go-Getters? Red flags went up all over the place in Polly's mind, but she couldn't quite figure out how to explain her reservations to the other teachers without confessing her attraction to Sam Goodacre.

"They need extra sponsors and a little bird...three of them, actually, told us you'd be the perfect one to ask to pitch in," Brianna summed up.

"You do have a dog, after all," Katie rushed to add. "And unless you just gave him a bath last night..."

"No, I haven't bathed him since…" The image of Sam sitting on the bathroom floor rubbing a towel over the dog's back while the little guy tried to lick his face filled Polly with the sweetest warmth tinged with sadness. "Um, no, he hasn't had a bath lately."

"Perfect. You can set the example for everyone, you know, to get them started." Brianna came to Polly's desk and wrote down the time, underlined, then circled it.

Polly chewed her lower lip. This was it. Her invitation to be a part of the community.

"What do you say?" Katie asked.

What could she say? The weekend stretched out before her and for the first time she realized she couldn't go "home," not now, or she'd never really *be* home in Baconburg. And the truth was, she *was* the perfect one for this particular job. She had the time. She had a special interest in watching over Caroline's progress or lack of it. And she had a dog that needed washing…again.

"What do I say? I say—" she picked up the piece of paper, folded it and tucked it into her purse "—I'll be there."

Out in the hallway giggles rose, then faded with the sounds of small feet hurrying away.

Polly clutched her purse to her chest and sighed. She had moved to a small town because she craved the slower pace, but Polly couldn't help thinking those triplets had just pulled a fast one on her.

"This is Caroline's day, girls." Sam waved to Juliette and Hayley from the drive while they waited on the porch pouting. This was his plan, the new-and-improved version. He wouldn't just push Caroline to find things to help her forge ahead; he'd use this as an opportunity to give her some special attention. So much for Polly's concerns about his not allowing Caroline to explore her individuality. "It's Caroline's club. Her fundraiser."

"Her plan," Gina muttered as she tucked Caroline into the passenger seat and double-checked that her seat belt fit properly.

"What?" Sam glared at his sister over the top of the minivan's hood.

"You don't think she's all excited to spend her Saturday morning washing just *any* old dog, do you?" Gina laughed and shook her head. "No wonder it was so easy to get you to volunteer to be a parent sponsor."

"Nobody 'got' me to volunteer. I'm doing this to support Caroline and…" And that's when Gina's point hit him. He thought about swapping kid duties with his sister, to have her attend the event and let him take charge at home. He glanced inside the car at Caroline. "Miss Bennett is going to be at this deal, I take it."

"Just give in and make the most of it, old man. Invite Polly and Donut out to the house for our barbecue Monday," Gina called out as she walked toward the house, not even looking back as if his agreement was a foregone conclusion.

"*Your* barbecue," he corrected, realizing that if he didn't take Caroline to the Go-Getters dog wash Gina would just make sure Polly and the pup made it out here for the holiday get-together. "*I'm* just going to hang around for the food and if you need any heavy lifting. Besides, I thought that barbecue was for the people helping you run the Pumpkin Jump. Polly's not in that group. Doesn't make sense to invite her."

"Makes perfect sense to me," Gina shouted at him from the porch.

"Us, too," Juliette and Hayley mimicked her.

"Let's go, Daddy!" Caroline kicked her feet and beamed at him. He hadn't gotten a smile that big out of her or heard her that excited to do anything in a long time.

"I have to go," he concluded. *Have* to, not *want* to. As he'd pointed out to Polly, you can't really hide in a small town. The sooner he crossed paths with the pretty teacher again, the better. From then on, it would be smooth sailing, right?

"Let's do this, kiddo," he said as he slid behind the wheel and started the van. "Full speed ahead."

Minutes later they parked behind the drugstore and headed through the drugstore as a shortcut to the firehouse, just down the block.

"I can go in your place and you can stay here to mind the store and try to figure out how to install this countertop if you—"

"No, thanks." Sam didn't allow his brother's offer to break his momentum as they passed through the store toward their destination. "We have a job to do."

That's how Sam decided to play it. Giving Caroline the best start was his job and that included sometimes interacting with Polly.

The fire chief directed everyone where to drop off kids, where to park and where the children should gather for instructions. Sam searched the scene, just to scope things out. One long table piled with poster board, paint, dog shampoo and a metal cashbox. Two bright blue plastic kiddie pools set up alongside the firehouse. Two firemen and the town's one firewoman filling those pools with water.

Caroline tugged at his arm. "Do you see them, Daddy?"

"See who?" He swept his gaze along the crowd, still trying to find a certain energetic young woman. It wasn't an emotional thing. Polly was just a teacher, just another partner in his plan to do the right thing for his girls. Nothing about this was personal.

His gaze landed on a knot of kids. A flash of black hair at the center, then a soft woof and Sam smiled. In a few steps, with Caroline keeping up pace for pace, he reached the cluster of children oohing, giggling and petting a golden-brown dog held in the arms of the prettiest teacher with no personal connection to him that he'd ever seen.

"Hi," she said to him softly as he stopped a few feet away from her.

"Hey." He gave her a nod. "You might have made more money for the cause charging tickets to pet that little guy, not to have the Go-Getters wash *other* people's dogs."

Polly shook her head. "He's not really mine."

The dog squirmed and licked her nose.

She made a face and laughed.

The children squealed, then the fire chief called them over for instructions on how to conduct themselves around the firehouse. They straggled off, although Caroline lingered longer than the others.

Polly looked sheepishly up at Sam, her face flushed. "I really have tried to find him a home."

"Looks to me like he found his *own* home." Sam crouched, putting his eyes level with Polly's. He stroked the dog's head just as the animal lifted it, trapping Sam's hand against Polly's cheek.

Their eyes met. His chest tightened. *Nothing personal,* he reminded himself.

The dog moved again and Sam slid his hand free.

Polly shut her eyes, then looked down. "I don't want you to think I haven't tried to keep my promise. But it just doesn't seem like anyone wants him."

"*I* want him," Caroline protested, throwing her arms around the dog's neck. "And I know Juliette and Hayley want him, too!"

Sam winced.

"Well, actually, Caroline, I'm thinking that maybe *I* might want him, after all." Polly came to his rescue.

"That's okay," Caroline shot back instantly. "If you take Donut we can still see him all the time, right?"

Polly fixed her big eyes on his face. The blush of color that had flooded her cheeks drained.

Sam wanted to rush to her rescue in return, but he hesitated. What could he say that wouldn't threaten his rules, wouldn't interfere with his plans? Was giving in to this going to stall any progress he might have made with Caroline, keep her too connected to the past?

"Okay, Caroline, enough for now." Sam played it safe. It was the right thing to do for his daughter, and to stick to his no-matchmaking rule. He could not promise to see Polly whenever his girls wanted a Donut fix. Things just didn't work that way. He gave her a smile and started to stand.

Polly stood up at the same time, faltering slightly when the dog in her arms wriggled.

Sam reached out to steady her, his heart thundering so hard it actually muffled the world surrounding the two of them for a moment.

"Hey, Grover! Hey there, boy!" A smiling brunette woman in blue work pants and a T-shirt with the Baconburg Fire Department insignia on it pointed toward Polly and the dog.

Polly shot Sam a look that he could only call pure panic.

He put his hand on his daughter's shoulder and gave her a nudge. "Go on, Caroline, you need to go listen to what the fire chief is saying."

"But I don't really want to." Caroline dragged her feet.

"Some things aren't about what we want," Sam told his daughter, although he kept his eyes on Polly, letting her know her messages to him hadn't gone unheeded. "I know you don't really want to be a Go-Getter, but the fact is, you signed up for it and for this event, and you need to honor your commitment." As Caroline reluctantly headed off to hear the instructions, Polly turned to face the firewoman who had called out to her, and squared her shoulders.

At that moment Sam realized he couldn't keep telling himself that things between him and Polly weren't personal. He may have known her only a short time, but that was more than long enough to sense the pain in her past. He'd have given just about anything to spare her any more.

He put his arm around her to lend whatever comfort and support he could. He raised his hand and called out to the woman who kept glancing their way as she finished filling the kiddie pool. "Hey, Angela! You, uh, you talking to Polly's dog?"

"I don't know Polly, but I do know Grover. It's so cool you brought him to the dog wash." She finished up her work and jogged toward them with her hand extended. "You must be Polly. You Ted's neighbor? Oh, or maybe…you're not…*the* girl?"

"*The* girl? No, I don't think so," she said with a quiet bravery that the slight tremble in her shoulders belied. "I don't see how I could be *the* girl because I don't know any Ted."

"You're not the girl Ted wanted to impress by getting a dog?" Angela stopped and put her hand over her mouth. "Oops. Maybe I wasn't supposed to say that. I'm a cat person myself, but I still don't get it. Ted's a great guy, really, but I don't see getting a dog for any other reason than love, do you?"

"No," Sam said in a firm, calm voice when Polly couldn't seem to find hers. He kept his arm lightly around her. "I can't see any reason at all, except love."

Polly tipped her head back to look up from beside him.

Sam did not meet her gaze. He just couldn't. He *could* forge ahead, though, get some answers, maybe clear up any questions so Polly wouldn't dwell on the worst. "So what makes you think this is Ted's dog? Is he missing?"

"I don't know. Ted's out of town until next Thursday for some specialized training." The brunette came toward them again with an assured spring in her steps. When she got close enough, she reached out and scratched behind the dog's ear. "I assumed he had put the dog in a kennel or had a friend watch it. This is absolutely his dog!"

Chapter Ten

"*Grover! Gro-o-over.* Grover?" Each time Polly called a variation on the name, the dog wagged his tail.

With the dog wash in full swing and Polly's emotions clearly on a roller coaster, Sam had suggested the two of them head to the drugstore to pick up cold soft drinks as a reward for the Go-Getters.

It only made sense to bring the dog, especially when they hung a sign on his back that read A Clean Dog Is a Happy Dog with info on the dog wash under that.

Polly eased the sign off the dog, then slumped on the floor, leaning back against the refrigerated drink unit. She gazed into the dog's eyes, patted his head and sighed. "I can't deny it. He does seem to like that name."

"Don't read too much into it." Sam let the drink-case door fall shut. He came to her side and offered her an ice-cold bottled water and some consolation. "I think he likes the person saying his name."

She managed an unconvincing smile as she reached up to take the drink.

He braced himself for the little emotional jolt he

always felt whenever their hands touched. And for the wave of regret that would follow when Polly would almost instantly withdraw shyly.

Only this time she didn't pull away.

Sam didn't exactly know what to feel or do about that. So he stood there looking down at her, his fingers practically entwined with hers. She had taken the news of potentially finding the dog's original owner in stride. Tried to pretend it was a good thing, even. Sam wanted to play along with that.

Why wouldn't he? It was what he'd have done. Looked at the new development as something to be accepted and moved past. It didn't hurt that it occurred to him that with the dog safely back in his first home that he and Polly could start to cultivate a workable relationship, meaning maybe they could be friends. Maybe even more, one day, when the girls were older.

"At least he's a firefighter. That generally means he's a good guy, right?" Her hand still on the drink he hadn't turned loose, she looked up at him with tears shimmering in her eyes above her wavering smile.

Who was he kidding? They were already past starting a workable friendship. Polly Bennett mattered to him. And if that meant taking her dog and all…

"I'd like to think so, but let's look at this a minute." Sam crouched down, surprising himself with the line of reasoning he was about to launch. "Angela Bodine couldn't tell us for sure that Ted's dog had even gone missing."

"She was fairly certain it was Ted's dog, though."

"Yeah, but you won't know until we talk to the neighbor and find out if that dog is missing, right?"

Sam smiled knowing that while Angela had given Polly the name of the neighbor she thought was supposed to be minding the dog Ted called Grover, Sam had taken a minute to get Ted's cell-phone number from one of the other firemen. Yes, Sam had a plan, and this time it wasn't about propelling his own agenda, but about protecting Polly.

She shrugged, her finger flexing against the plastic bottle. The fact that she had not taken the drink told Sam that despite her seeming indifference, she was still listening.

"So, why are you, of all people, rushing to a conclusion?" He lowered his head, seeking to keep her eyes on his. "Angela said this Ted guy got the dog to impress a girl and had only had the animal a week before he volunteered to go to specialty training school."

"Yes, so?" Polly nodded and tugged the bottle toward her at last.

Sam tugged back to keep his hold. "So technically by the time he gets back, you will both have had the dog roughly the same amount of time. Plus he left the dog with an unreliable caregiver."

Another nod. Another tug.

Sam took a deep breath and let go of the bottle as he looked into her eyes and grinned. "So don't get in such an all-fired hurry to give up, Miss Bennett. You should know that. Give it time to see how it works out. You may be pleasantly surprised."

Her smile trembled, then grew. She looked down, laughed and shook her head. The dog in her lap licked her chin. "Did you hear that, Donut or Grover or whatever your name ends up being? Mr. Just Keep Moving Forward thinks time might be on our side."

Sam had to laugh, too. If he hadn't said it himself, he'd have never believed it. He stood and offered his hand to her. "But for now, we've got to get these drinks over to the kids."

She got up without his help, brushed off her jeans, then pulled on the leash to get the dog to cooperate. A deep breath. A swig of water. She squared her shoulders and headed for the door, but just before she opened it for Sam, who had a box filled with bottled drinks, she looked back. "I just don't know how I'm going to fill the time between now and when I find out what happens next."

"I have a suggestion!" Max's voice came practically bouncing off the walls from the back of the store.

"Didn't anyone ever tell you it's rude to listen in on other people's conversations?" Sam hoisted the heavy box high against his chest.

"Yeah, you'd have thought my older brother would have taught me stuff like that but he's pretty rude, too—not inviting the pretty new teacher to—"

"I was getting to it," Sam hollered back before looking down at Polly as he brushed past her. "I really was."

Yeah, he'd told Gina it wasn't a good idea, but that was before Polly had looked so vulnerable, so much as if she needed a friend. He wouldn't let himself be more for now, but he could be that much, couldn't he? "Why don't you come out to the house for the Pumpkin Jump planning-committee appreciation barbecue Monday? If you can stand more of Max's cooking."

"Pumpkin Jump?" Polly stepped out into the sunshine and shaded her eyes, but under the shade she created she wore a playful smile. "Are you just making that up to take my mind off Ted Perry?"

"Much as I'd love to take credit for anything that takes your mind off another man…" He could have worded that a little more, uh, *friend*ish. He cleared his throat. "Off the situation with Donut, or Grover or—"

"I get it," she said softly, her smile soft and sweet.

"Please come out to the house Monday." He clutched the box and held his ground until he got an answer, ready to stay put until he got the answer he wanted. "Bring Donut. Around three?"

She walked past him to check traffic, and motioned him to follow her into the street. "I'll think about it."

Like so many things where Polly was concerned, Sam's plan did not work out as he'd expected and she left him no way to just push through to get his way. He shook his head and followed along, laughing at himself softly as he added, "I guess that's all a guy can ask for."

The rest of the event went by quickly. She and Sam agreed not to tell Caroline and the other girls about the new development until they had more solid information. Polly tried to wheedle more about this Ted Perry from Angela—and the allegedly negligent neighbor he had left his pet with—without seeming as if she was trying to find out about him. She stayed upbeat. She cheered on the Go-Getters. She waved signs to draw in customers. In other words, she was pretty much just herself, even though it took a lot of effort to do so and to keep Sam from knowing how anxious this all made her.

She had begun to like coming home to the little dog after work and certainly didn't mind having another living thing in the house at night. She had come to Baconburg to create a life she thought would make her happy, make her finally feel she belonged. Donut had helped her begin to do that. Now she imagined taking a photo of the little golden-brown dog and sitting it up on the mantel with all the other loved ones absent from her life.

Polly glanced across the firehouse drive to see Sam prodding Caroline step by step to keep helping the others clean up after themselves. The day she had found the man in front of her new house she had felt so confident that she stood on the very verge of her small-town dreams of friends, family and home coming true.

No dogs. No matchmaking. The man's rules echoed through her thoughts.

Polly's stomach knotted at how quickly her big dream of a new life grew smaller and smaller every day. She had come all this way and it seemed she hadn't really found or gained a thing.

"C'mon, Donut. Let's go home and wait for Ted Perry or his neighbor's phone call." She turned away from the firehouse.

"Hey, Polly, um, that is, Miss Bennett!" Pounding footsteps accompanied Sam's voice. "You can't run away now."

Polly tensed at the phrase that echoed Essie's assessment of Polly's behavior. But she couldn't deny it; Sam was right. She needed to stay and see this through as an example to the kids and to honor her commitment, no matter how disenchanted she had become with life in Baconburg so far.

She tugged on the leash and turned around saying, "Sorry, Donut, we still have to—"

"Hop on!" Sam motioned to her from the second row of seats inside a shiny yellow fire truck.

"What? What's this?" Polly blinked.

"For a job well-done." Angela, the lady firefighter, leaned over the driver and motioned to Polly to get on board.

"And a last grab for donations," Sam added as he leaned down with his hand extended to her. "The Go-Getters and their sponsors get a ride down Main Street on the fire truck."

Polly hesitated. "But Donut…"

"Hey, dogs and fire trucks are a natural," the fireman behind the wheel shouted. "Bring the little guy along. He'll be a great nudge for people to fill our boots with cash."

"You can help, too!" Angela hoisted up a big, black rubber boot with yellow reflective-tape trim.

"People will feel especially happy to help make our favorite new Baconburg-ite and schoolteacher feel at home."

Polly laughed, the weight on her shoulders and in her heart lifting at least a little. Here was her invitation to be a part of this place, to stop running and be at home. That it came from Sam's lips didn't hurt.

She scooped up the dog and handed him up to Sam and Caroline, then climbed on herself. With the sun on her face, and Sam and Caroline and Donut at her side, all her cares and concerns melted away. She shut her eyes and in her heart made a prayer of gratitude.

"Not in my time, but in Yours," she whispered. She didn't control how fast or slow things went by dragging her feet or moving to a new place any more than Sam did by pressing relentlessly onward.

She opened her eyes and looked at him holding Caroline in his lap, and her with Donut in hers. The man was so full of surprises. If only he could see how happy his daughter looked right now, just being herself, being with him, maybe he'd back off trying to make the child conform to his expectations. Polly grabbed her cell phone and captured the moment.

"Now you take one of Miss Bennett, Daddy," Caroline urged.

"My hands are full. Besides, there'll be time for pictures on Monday," he said before he dropped a kiss on his daughter's head, endured a lick from the dog in her arms, then met Polly's gaze and smiled. "Miss Bennett is coming out for the barbecue with us, right, Miss Bennett?"

It was totally unfair means for him to get his way. And it worked.

Polly took a breath, pressed the button to save the photo in her phone and laughed. "Right. Okay, I'll be there."

Maybe he'd listened in or maybe he was just entertaining the kids, but just then the fireman driving let the siren go.

Polly's gaze met Sam's, and she knew deep down that the sudden blaring sound was not the only reason her heart rate had begun to race.

Chapter Eleven

Polly and Donut made the drive out to Goodacre Organic Farm without incident. If you didn't count reconsidering the wisdom of spending the day with Sam and his family...all right, mostly Sam...so much that she almost turned around twice a non-incident. The second time she thought about not going ahead, her cell phone rang. That gave her the perfect excuse to pull over to the side of the road.

"Hello?" Maybe the barbecue had been called off. She squelched the silly thought as soon as it popped into her head.

Actually, it turned out she would have liked that turn of events better than the news she got.

"Of course, of course," she found herself saying to conclude the short, slightly panicky conversation with Ted Perry's neighbor because she didn't know how to say what she really wanted to say. "Of course I can bring him over. Tomorrow? After school?"

She clicked the button to end the call, then stole a peek over her shoulder at Donut. "She says she checked the dog pound daily and didn't see any of the flyers. I think she saw them and thought I'd make a convenient dogsitter until somebody Ted works with saw you."

The dog's thick tail beat against the side of the carrier.

The sound echoed the heavy pounding of Polly's heart. She thought of calling the Goodacres and canceling, but she'd told the neighbor she couldn't bring Donut over because she was on her way to a party. So if she didn't go, she'd need to give the dog back sooner. A lump rose in Polly's throat. She didn't know when she had ever felt so alone.

She grabbed the keys to start the car again, but reached for the phone instead and called her sister, Essie.

"I should have known I'd get your voice mail." Polly *had* known, if she were honest with herself. She had probably wanted to get it, in fact. Just hearing her sister's voice eased her jangled nerves. And if her sister had actually answered, Polly probably would never have had the gumption to speak her heart as she did. "I miss you. I miss the whole family, but you especially. And not just because of your cooking because Sam, you remember Sam? The widower whose hat I ran over? Well, he has a brother who is cooking today. So I am covered in the getting-fed-without-eating-my-own-cooking department."

Polly clenched her teeth and paused to keep her voice from breaking. "Listen to me, stalling, when what I really want to do is pour my whole heart out to you. Essie, I really thought I was making a good move coming here. That I'd finally find my way, but I am so afraid I'm not fitting in here, and if I don't fit here and I don't fit in Atlanta, then..."

An electronic beep on the line told her she'd run out of time. She gazed at her phone and contemplated calling again to finish her thought. Or recant it. She didn't want her family to worry.

After a moment, she decided to leave it as it was. Essie would understand and in a way only a sister could. Polly started the car again, then checked the clock in the dashboard.

"Oh, great. On top of everything else, the new girl is going to be late!" She hit the gas and took off down the vacant road. The rural countryside that had reminded her on her first trip out to the farm of quaint paintings and photos from calendars whizzed past. She didn't waste a minute admiring those kinds of scenes.

"What?" she asked the dog, who was safely tucked into a borrowed carrier in the backseat. "Peace? Acceptance? Happiness? I've chased it so long without a real definition of what I've wanted out of life that I'm not sure I'd even recognize it if I ran into it."

Sam's poor hat. Her thoughts raced faster than her quiet little hybrid car, jumping from her concerns to her desire to make a good impression to the still-crumpled hat sitting in her kitchen. She really had to get that taken care of. Not that he seemed to miss it. "That's the thing, though, isn't it? The fact that he acts like he doesn't care about it, this whole get-over-it, keep-moving-forward attitude of his? I don't buy it."

A quick, sharp woof seemed to ring out in agreement.

Before she could compliment her canine companion

on his obvious people skills, Polly heard the voices of the triplets behind her. How was she going to tell them about the neighbor wanting Donut back?

"Wait! The *triplets?*" She hit the brakes. She had completely missed the driveway where they were standing waving their arms.

She'd come out here today as a comforting distraction, but in doing so, had she just employed Sam's just-keep-pushing-onward strategy? Was she becoming more like her own family and Sam's ideal of a family than becoming her own woman? The notion gave her a shiver.

She backed up slowly, careful of the three girls jumping up and down and calling, "Miss Bennett! Miss Bennett!"

Polly motioned for the girls to stay clear as she parked at the end of a row of vehicles. Suddenly she wondered how many people would be there, and what they would think of the new teacher being invited out by the local most-eligible single dad? She just managed to get out but not to get into the backseat to let Donut out of his carrier when the girls surrounded her.

"We've been waiting for you, Miss Bennett!" Juliette clapped her hands and jumped up and down.

"Hurry up and come with us." Hayley pointed to the band of wide gravel intended for farm visitors' vehicles. "We have a lot to get done!"

"What is it with you Goodacres? In the South we at least take a minute to welcome our guests before we put them to work." She meant it to sound teasing, not scolding, but as Juliette and Hayley hurried off, Polly began thinking of a way to make sure they knew she wasn't mad.

She shut her eyes and drew in a deep breath and then heard a small, sweet voice.

"Did you bring Donut?" Caroline rose up on tiptoes as if she might catch a glimpse in the car. "Daddy told us that the lady firefighter thinks she knows his other owner. Do you still have him?"

"He's right here." Polly put her hand on the girl's back reassuringly as she reached for the car door handle.

Caroline looked up at Polly, her brown eyes somber but filled with hope. "Can I help take care of him today while everyone does stuff?"

One last time. The little girl didn't say it but it was in her tone. That, on the heels of the call Polly had made to Essie, cut right through to Polly's heart. In that moment she felt not much older than the triplets herself.

The memory of being the sister who always lagged behind welled up within her. Deep down, Polly was still the one whose dreams seemed small and unambitious, her skills and accomplishments never measuring up to her twin's, the one whose simple plans never quite came true. If there was any way she could help Caroline grow up without that legacy, Polly determined she would do it.

She could start by giving Caroline something to take pride in, being the one Polly trusted with this important task. "It's okay with me if it's okay with your dad."

They got the dog out and while Polly did hold the

leash, Caroline kept her hand on it, too, and marched along at Donut's side. They followed Hayley and Juliette's path to the back part of the farmhouse and straight into a scene of chaos already in progress.

Gina, standing beside a large paper flip chart with all sorts of frantic-looking scribbles on it, waved a large black marker in her direction. "We're divvying up assignments. This is everyone who's going to run games, booths, parking or sell food, for the Pumpkin Jump. Everyone, this is Polly Bennett."

The half dozen or so people seated at the long picnic table in front of her all turned their heads to peer at the late arrival.

"Hi." Polly tried to wave and ended up slapping herself in the knee with the dog leash.

The group didn't seem to notice. They waved, and some called out, "Hi, Polly."

"Miss Bennett, Miss Bennett!" Juliette and Hayley all but did acrobatics to draw her attention. "Everyone has stuff to do! You can do something with us, too, if you want."

Max stepped away from the large brick barbecue and gave a salute with long silver tongs. "Juliette, Hayley and I could use some help here. We've got platters of burgers and hotdogs to grill. Or you can help my grumpy old brother collect some pumpkins for the committee photo. I have to warn you, though, *that's* not the glam job it sounds like."

"Yep, it's just me, a field and a little red wagon." Sam came wheeling out a child's wagon with slatted sides. He let the handle drop and bounce off the sidewalk.

The group groaned.

Gina shook her head.

"No fair playing the pity card, old man." Max brandished the tongs with a flourish. "Although of the two of us, you probably do need the most help, lifting those heavy pumpkins and getting them back to the house."

"Yeah, yeah. Walking and lifting and working in the fields isn't nearly as hard as flipping burgers." Sam gave his brother a snort, then rolled his sleeves up over his forearms and elbows, exposing the bulge of his tanned biceps. "But you're welcome to tag along if you like, Polly."

All eyes fixed on her just in time to catch her stealing an admiring glance at Sam's strong arms.

"Oh, I don't know about that." She quickly looked away and cleared her throat, trying to match her tone to the light banter between the brothers. "It might not seem proper, the new schoolmarm going off into the pumpkin patch with a man and his little red wagon."

As soon as the words left her lips it struck her that they might sound more flirtatious than funny, more so when she scanned the amused expressions of the people around her. One of whom—Max, Gina, one or all of the triplets—might have seen her and Sam kissing in the upstairs hallway not all that long ago! Polly started to explain, couldn't find the words and so sank down to sit on the edge of one of the picnic benches on the patio, hoping it looked as if she meant to do so.

"Smart girl." Max started to head toward her with his hand out to guide her to the barbecue area. "Better to stay where there are plenty of chaperones."

"Or take your own along," Gina called out. "Take Donut."

The dog's whole body wriggled at the sound of the name. In a heartbeat he slipped away from Polly's grasp and ran right up to Sam, who dropped down on one knee to stop him.

Caroline rushed up and tugged at Polly's hand to get the teacher on her feet again. "You said I could take care of Donut today, so can I go, too?"

Polly staggered a step with Caroline pulling her, then paused and gathered enough composure to walk over to Sam. "What do you think?"

Sam hesitated.

Polly gazed down at him on bended knee before her for a moment longer than she probably should have before she realized everyone was watching. She leaned down then to grab up the dog's leash again, using that movement to whisper to Sam, "I just got off the phone with Ted Perry's neighbor. She wants me to return the dog tomorrow."

Sam pulled back and met her gaze.

Polly didn't want to look him in the eyes. She wasn't ready, and she knew his gaze would reveal how disappointed this turn of events made her feel.

He stood up and gave her hand a squeeze before turning to take up the wagon handle again and starting off. After only a couple of steps, he looked back at Polly and Caroline. "Well? What are you waiting for?" He motioned for them to follow him. "Let's go."

Polly went along, promising the other triplets she'd make time for them later. She launched into a conversation with Sam that began loudly enough for everyone to hear it was purely platonic. "So, I have yet to hear a serious explanation of this 'Pumpkin Jump' deal. What is it exactly? Do you have a contest to see who can jump over the most pumpkins in a row? Or one by one like leapfrog? Or is it more like pole-vaulting to see who can clear the largest pumpkin?"

Caroline giggled at the empty chatter and ran ahead down the path away from the house.

"No, no and no." Sam laughed and shook his head.

Gradually the farmhouse grew smaller behind them and the long rows of vines and pumpkins surrounded by long, low stone walls came into view.

Polly stopped to take in the sight for a moment, her thoughts filled with the words of Ecclesiastes. *To everything there is a season...*

For a split second it all seemed right again. Just for now she had friends and Donut and the beauty of a day with them when the sun was low and the shadows long and she didn't have to rush anywhere or compete for anything. "This is just like I imagined it would be."

"You *imagined* our farm?" Sam stopped to turn back to face Polly.

Caroline took advantage of that to load Donut into the wagon and hop in beside him herself.

"I imagined my life," she corrected, her heart halfway between nostalgia over her naïveté and shyness at revealing something so personal. "When my parents split up and I never seemed to be able to keep up with all their activities and expectations, I imagined there was a place where seeds were planted and nurtured and simply allowed to grow into what they were meant to be."

"Are you talking about people or pumpkins?" Caroline asked, clearly not sure what Polly was driving at.

"Both. That is, I'm taking about how in the years after my family moved away from Baconburg, I couldn't help remembering it as a place where people moved at their own pace." She raised her head slightly to find Sam and Caroline, and even Donut, staring at her. Heat rose in her cheeks. She hooked her thumbs in her belt loops and gave a one-sided shrug. "And when the time came those people weren't afraid to jump over a few pumpkins!"

"Leaves!" Caroline shouted even as she laughed at Polly turning her heartfelt vision into an act to keep from feeling she'd revealed too much.

"What?" Polly cocked her head. "You want me to leave?"

"Leaves. You know, that change color and fall from the trees every autumn?" The golden rays of sun highlighted the crinkles around Sam's smiling eyes as he held open the wooden gate in the wall for her. "We rake up all the leaves around here and haul them into huge piles in the yard. That's what we jump into."

"We?" she asked as she moved past Sam through the opening, so close that the sleeve of her lightweight summer sweater brushed the pearl buttons of his cotton shirt. "*You* jump in piles of leaves? I'd like to see that."

"Me, too," Caroline announced. Obviously impatient with not going anywhere, the pint-size redhead jumped out, grabbed the leash and pushed her way between the two of them with Donut in tow. "Only Daddy hasn't done it since back when Mommy got sick. Us girls don't even remember it."

Sam's whole body tensed.

Polly sank her teeth into her lower lip to keep from impulsively blurting out an observation about the ruined hat, the ridiculous rules or what price he might be paying for pushing his kids to move on before they were ready. Just before she joined Caroline and Donut on the quest for the best-looking pumpkins, she said, "To everything there is a season, Sam. You can't make Caroline bloom on your schedule any more than you can make these pumpkin vines produce on cue."

Chapter Twelve

"Actually you *can* force a flower to bloom *and* affect the growth of crops. That's how they get those monster pumpkins." Sam winced at how childish he sounded. He had known what Polly meant. The fact that he fully understood it was probably the very reason he reacted as he did.

To his relief Polly had already hurried along after Caroline and Donut. She didn't seem to have heard his argumentative tone as she tipped her head to one side to listen intently to his daughter, who had stopped to admire a lopsided, squatty pumpkin. They made a nice scene standing there in the fields of this farm that he loved. Polly looked good here, looked right.

The little dog leaped about and barked, and suddenly Sam couldn't help thinking how the girls would react to the news of Donut going away. He gripped the cold metal handle of the wagon. Maybe if things were different. But Sam knew that unlike Polly he did not have the luxury of imagining a world the way he wished it could be and then running off to try to re-create it. He had to deal with the realities of three little girls who had already lost too much and could not afford to lose anything else.

"Let's get this over with. Just point out the ones you want and I'll load 'em in the wagon." Sam reached them in a few long strides and parked the wagon. The handle fell into the dirt with a clatter and a clank. "Gina said we need at least three, but I think six this size will fit."

"Uh-uh." Caroline waved her hand through the air and took off running down the row. Donut bounded along behind her with his ears flapping and his leash flying.

"Uh-uh?" He looked to Polly for a translation.

"She says it's too…" Polly crinkled up her adorable nose, pursed her lips, then puffed out her cheeks.

"Too…" Sam tried his best to imitate the face Polly had just made.

Polly burst out laughing at his attempt, then shook her head. "She says she'll know what she wants when she sees it."

Sam tipped his head back and groaned. "We may be out here until dusk."

"Are we in a time crunch?"

I am, he wanted to say. *I can't spend any longer here with you than is necessary because you and Donut are not a part of our future.*

Polly shaded her eyes, her face turned his way. "Well?"

"I guess not," Sam admitted grudgingly. "They still have a lot to accomplish with the committee and the grill wasn't even ready when we left."

"Do you think Max needs our help?" She folded her

arms in what a kid might have seen as a teacherly way, challenging him to thoroughly examine the situation and come to the best conclusion.

Sam couldn't help himself—future or not, he just saw her trying to guide him around to her line of thinking as charming.

There were worse things, he decided, than spending a few extra minutes of his day with Polly. And with Caroline, he was quick to remind himself. They were here to see what they could do to help Caroline have the most successful school year possible. Letting the child take the lead here might even finally show Polly what he was up against in getting the girl to make decisions and put them into action. That was what he needed to focus on. He cleared his throat and squinted across the field back toward the house, then looked at Polly again.

She had not budged. He probably should have seen that as a sign that she would not be easily swayed. But all he saw was how the breeze ruffled her perpetually ruffled-looking hair. How the sunlight warmed the healthy glow in her cheeks. How her lips, even pressed tightly together as if warning him to think carefully about how he proceeded, seemed so kissable.

"Max will clang the dinner bell when the burgers are done, so until then…" He bent slightly and held his hand out as if offering her the breadth and width of the Goodacre pumpkin patch.

"Until then…" She did a little sashay of a step past him and started after Caroline.

Sam tried to throw himself into the spirit of the outing. He really did. Time after time he bent to gather up what seemed like a perfectly acceptable pumpkin only to have Caroline reject it before Sam could settle it into the wagon. Each was deemed too bumpy or too lumpy or not pumpkiny enough.

"Now, this—" Sam said as he pointed to a tall, oblong and flawlessly orange specimen "—*this* is the model pumpkin. In fact, one might call it the super-model of pumpkins."

Caroline frowned. "It's kinda skinny."

"Don't make up your mind until you see it on the runway." Sam abandoned the still-empty wagon, grabbed up the pumpkin he'd picked out and hoisted it up on his shoulder. He walked away, then did a turn to the delight of his little girl, and the obvious amusement of her pretty teacher, and walked back toward them. "And remember, the camera adds ten pounds."

"So that would make it look like twice its size?" Polly said with a smile.

"Hey, we're talking supermodel, not super math genius here." He grinned back at Polly, then lowered the pumpkin just above the wagon. "What do you say, kiddo, do we finally have a keeper?"

Caroline squinted hard. Her mouth scrunched up on one side.

Sam waited as patiently as he could possibly manage for five, ten, fifteen seconds, then exhaled. "Caroline, honey, it's just a snapshot on the farm's webpage. People will never notice a few imperfections."

Caroline lowered her gaze, then curled her hands into fists and looked across the way. "I think I see a better one a couple rows over."

And off she went, just a blur of red hair and golden dog, barking behind her.

Sam shut his eyes and clenched his jaw. "Do you see now why I feel I have to give her a nudge now and then to get her moving in the right—no, scratch that—in *any* direction?"

"Maybe she's the kind who needs a little longer to find her *own* direction?" Polly tried to tuck a strand of hair behind her ear, but the wind whipped it right back across her face.

Sam studied her for a moment. A day ago he had wondered how Polly's input on raising the girls might compare to Marie's. Now he wondered if Polly really understood his girls and him at all.

"Hayley and Juliette aren't like that. I can't hold them back." Even if chasing after them from one extracurricular activity to the next wore him thin, Sam refused to see that as a bad thing. "I'm afraid if I don't lay down the law with Caroline she'll just drift along, or keep waiting until everything is perfect to make her move. If I don't push her to push herself to meet a few basic expectations *now* she'll never do anything."

Polly ignored the hair pressed by the sweep of the wind to her cheek, shaded her eyes and watched the girl walking slowly around a plump, round pumpkin.

"Did you ever think that maybe she *is* doing something, Sam?" Polly took a few steps toward the girl, paused, then turned to him, her voice strained as spoke fast and heated. "Just because it's not what you'd do or what Juliette or Hayley would do does not mean it's nothing."

"Whoa!" He held up his hands in a sign of surrender. Only he wasn't surrendering. Not where his girls were concerned. "This is *my* family we're talking about here, Polly. Not some family you quilted together out of your memories."

"That was kind of harsh." Polly pulled her shoulders back. She blinked her big eyes at him, but she didn't shed a tear or sniffle. Her face went pale but she did not deny his observation. "I only wanted to help you see things from Caroline's point of view."

"You don't know Caroline's point of view, Polly." He kept his tone calm, almost comforting. He did not mean to hurt or humiliate her, just to hold his ground where his daughter was concerned. "You don't know what it means to have lost your mom so young, to know you'll grow up as a motherless girl. Or what it's like to have two sisters who could easily outshine you at every turn if you don't step up and grab a little of the spotlight yourself."

"I may not know Caroline's exact point of view, Sam, but don't presume you know enough about *me* to make those remarks." She lashed her hand through the air. "I actually have some pretty good insight into how it feels to have your family in pieces from a young age. I know what it is to always be in the shadow. I have some insight into at least some part of what Caroline is going through."

"Hey, you guys! I found one!" Caroline leaped in the air, her arms waving wildly. Above a barrage of excited barking, she put her hand to the side of her mouth and yelled, "I found a perfect pumpkin!"

"She's my daughter, Polly." Sam bent to take up the handle to the wagon and started toward the post Caroline had staked out. He was simply stating the facts as he saw them. "I think I know what's best for her."

Sam gathered up the pumpkin Caroline had singled out. Even he had to admit it looked far better than any of the previous choices and probably would make the best display of the farm's bounty on the webpage. From that point on she seemed on a hot streak, selecting another, then another until they had a wagon full of produce so round and orange that Polly observed, "If you hired an artist to make a painting to convey 'pumpkin' to people who had never seen a single one, the result wouldn't look any more pumpkin-rific than these. Just like professional book illustrators."

"Did you hear that, Donut? Professional book ill-o-stators!" Caroline beamed.

The dog wagged his tail as if impressed by this bit of news.

In the near distance a clanging from the back of the house sounded and Max called out, "Come and get it!"

"Cool!" Caroline surged ahead.

Donut started after her, then whipped his head around to look at Polly. She smiled at the small animal.

Sam half expected the bighearted educator to grab Donut and hug him as hard as she could. He held his breath, not sure what he would do if she reacted that way.

Polly only nodded and said quietly, "Go on, boy. It's okay."

The animal ran off, staying right at Caroline's heels.

Polly called out some instruction for Caroline not to let the dog bother anyone and to get him some water and so on. When the pair got out of hearing range, she sighed and looked at him. "Still friends?"

"I think we're mature enough to get past a difference of opinion now and then." Sam had to use both hands to tug the wagon over the rutted dip where the gate stood open.

"As long as I concede that you're right?" she added with a grin.

He didn't answer that. Instead he moved on to a topic he had wanted to broach all day. "So you going to be okay if it turns out you have to hand over the dog?"

"Me? You're worried about *me?*" She shook her head, then turned and, seeing him bogged down with his load, helped him wrangle the wheels up and over onto flat land. When they started to roll again, she said, "I was genuinely surprised you let Caroline spend so much time with him today."

Sam shifted his shoulders. A day's physical labor had them tight and aching, he decided, refusing to consider any other reason he'd be feeling tension during a simple, civil discussion with Polly. "Now that it's a very real possibility that he belongs to someone else, the dog is less of a…"

"Threat?" she supplied helpfully.

He didn't grin but he didn't frown, either. Instead he fixed his attention on not losing any off the pile of roly-poly pumpkins. "I was going to say 'distraction.'"

Polly stood her ground, arms folded, and pushed the limit of their fledgling friendship yet again. "Ah, you mean seeing Donut, or Grover as Ted Perry calls him, going back to his happy new home will provide a living, breathing, face-licking lesson in moving on without any of the mess of letting go or saying good-bye forever. Score a point for Sam's way."

He turned abruptly to face her, not sure what he would say because she was, essentially, right. He did think of the whole finding-the-dog's-owner situation, however it worked out, as a valuable lesson in just the kind of thing he'd tried so hard to instill in his girls. If the dog went with Ted, then Polly would move on and they'd see that. If the dog stayed with Polly, then…

"Miss Bennett! Miss Bennett!" Juliette, Hayley and Caroline came practically tumbling over each other down the hill straight for them. "Will you sit by me at dinner?" Hayley asked.

"No, me!" Juliette pleaded.

"Sit by me!" Caroline called.

"You got to spend the last hour with her," Hayley protested.

Sam squared his shoulders, set his jaw and began to pull the loaded wagon up the hill without another word.

"Is Daddy mad?" Caroline asked softly.

"No, I'm not mad," Sam shot back even as he forged ahead. "I just want to get this wagon unloaded."

"C'mon, girls, let's see what we can do to help your dad get that done." Polly came jogging up the hill to scoop one of the pumpkins up off the top of the heap. To Sam's surprise even one less made it easier going.

Next, Hayley and Juliette each came up and Polly used the toe of her shoe to point out the smallest of the bunch and the girls each took one.

"What can I do?" Caroline asked, peering at the remaining large pumpkins.

"Push," Polly told her.

So Caroline pushed and the wagon rolled along with much less effort from Sam.

"Things sure do get a lot easier when you work together instead of trying to stubbornly stick to your own way." Polly twirled around to walk backward for a moment as she added, "That sounds familiar. Where have I heard that?"

"Corinthians." Sam kept moving as he recited the familiar verse. "'Love is patient and kind. Love is not jealous or boastful or proud or rude. It does not demand its own way. It is not irritable, and it keeps no record of being wronged. It does not rejoice about injustice but rejoices whenever the truth wins out. Love never gives up, never loses faith, is always hopeful and endures through every circumstance.'"

Polly stood there with the group in the background and listened to him, her mouth slightly open as if she'd just watched him lift the wagon over his head and carry it one-handed up the hill.

"Impressed?" He grinned at her. "I memorized it to read when my parents renewed their vows a few years ago."

Her whole face had gone bright red. She looked away. "Boy, I sure am hungry."

"Really?" He only gave her a sideways look as he passed her on his way to join the group. "I'd have thought you'd be full already, after the bite you took out of me."

Caroline stopped in her tracks, her eyes big. "Miss Bennett! You *bit* my dad?"

Sam started to laugh, but Max beat him to it. The

rest of the group joined in and Sam couldn't help thinking that it was going to be a long time before he was able to move on from a remark like that.

Chapter Thirteen

Sam looked surprised by Caroline's loud proclamation for maybe a millisecond. He made an expression that seemed to say, *What just happened?*

Polly held her breath.

Sam cocked his head and narrowed his eyes at his child.

Everyone looked at him, then at Polly, then at him again.

Sam shrugged. Then he laughed.

The whole group joined in. Within a minute he had begun to pass pumpkins off to eager helpers as if nothing had happened.

It was the perfect way to handle it and Polly knew it the instant he did it. If it had been left up to her, she would probably have rushed headlong into some lengthy explanation of her having given him a piece of her mind and why she had done that and what she had meant by it all. Minutes would pass and maybe the group would have forgotten the "teacher bites dad" image in their heads, but only because her actions replaced that image with a "teacher puts foot in mouth, newcomer bites off more than she can chew" one.

With the wagon unloaded and the whole group on their feet, Gina asked Sam to say the blessing for their meal. Every head bowed.

"Dear Lord, I was just reminded of Ecclesiastes and Your design, that to everything there is a season. As we enter into this season of harvesting and celebration, of planting and planning for the future, the time for our children to learn and to grow, we ask Your blessing on those who have a hand in these things. For the farmers, the parents, the teachers, those who help in all aspects to support each other and love You. And as it says in Ecclesiastes, 'People should eat and drink and enjoy the fruits of their labor, for these are gifts from God.' Amen."

"Amen," the whole group said in unison.

"Amen," Polly whispered one beat behind.

Sam's way worked. Polly took a seat at the end of the picnic table and considered that as they enjoyed their meal.

The afternoon faded slowly into evening with the group sharing stories of Pumpkin Jumps past. It did not escape Polly's attention that each person there made a point of telling her a tale about Sam. The year Sam was thirteen and Max was nine and Sam wanted to keep Max busy, so he came up with a maze made of hay bales and when Max got lost and scared how Sam plowed straight through the walls of hay to Max's rescue. Then there was the story from a couple of years ago when the local weatherman had predicted an early snow for the day of the Jump, much to the girls' delight. When it didn't come, Sam spent half the night scouring the patch to collect the right-size pumpkins to stack up like three small "snowmen" to greet the girls in the morning. Time and again she heard the phrase "Nothing stops Sam."

Nothing stopped him, Polly thought, except his own rules, or his own reasons for sticking to those rules.

Sam reacted to the praise and teasing with humility and good humor until someone said, "You know, my favorite Sam story was the year he dressed up as 'Pumpkin Pete the Cowboy.' Marie laughed so much at the getup—"

Others laughed and nodded in agreement. "I think that's enough storytelling." Sam stood and clapped his hands together before anyone tried to elaborate. "The girls have school tomorrow and they have to get their baths, so if you'll all excuse us…"

Despite their groans and complaints Sam prodded the girls to go tell everyone goodbye and go into the house.

Polly watched in awe. She glanced from person to person, wondering why no one else seemed to notice. How could they have just been sharing those stories one minute and now getting up and going home the next? Didn't anyone see what had just happened?

They probably all assumed that was just Sam. He'd made up his mind and that was that. But didn't anyone else see that the time he decided to up and move on was the moment when he and the girls might have shared a moment remembering Marie Goodacre?

He called to Juliette not to try to tumble up the hill to the house and directed Hayley not to forget to clear away her dessert plate. Then he held his hand out to Caroline to bring her along.

A knot twisted in the pit of her stomach. She wished she had known this when she had confronted him earlier. It all seemed so clear now. Sam wasn't pushing his girls to move forward to the future so they wouldn't experience more loss. He was running away from having to deal with the pain of his own past.

If Polly understood anything it was running away. She glued her gaze to the man's back, took a deep breath and hopped up. "The girls aren't the only ones who have school tomorrow. I better go collect Donut and be on my way."

More protests from the girls even as they followed their father around to the front of the house. "Please, Miss Bennett, please, stay and read the Donut story to us."

Polly shook her head. She didn't think she could read Marie Goodacre's story tonight, written for those adorable girls about a dog who only wanted to be loved. Not after her words with Sam and the realization that he had not fully dealt with his wife's death. Not knowing she might have to give up both her dog and now her ideas about helping Caroline because she couldn't wait to blurt out her opinion. "I really shouldn't, girls. I can walk with you up to the house, though."

The whole way Juliette and Hayley vied for Polly's attention, which she happily lavished on them.

The handful of committee members who hadn't already gone home trailed along, calling out their goodbyes and thank-yous and began to leave as Polly got to the house.

"Donut is in the kitchen," Gina said as she pointed in the direction of the brightly lit room while herding the girls upstairs.

Polly thanked Gina for having her, and hurried to collect Donut and get back to the door. Before she left, she looked up the stairs and called out, "Good night, girls. I'll see you all tomorrow at…"

A torrent of water rushing through old pipes resonated from upstairs through the house.

"School." Polly looked around the dimly lit foyer. The hallway was dark, the living room silent. Light shone from the kitchen like a beacon. Sam's kitchen.

The last time she had been alone with him in this house, he'd kissed her. Of course, the last time she was alone with him outside the house she had scolded him. She put her fingertips to her lips, unsure what any of that meant. Unsure if she could face the man alone again…or if he was even in that kitchen.

She held her breath. She could do this. Whatever "this" became she could—

Essie's special ringtone cut off that thought, filling the foyer and seeming to ricochet all around the quiet, cozy home.

"Hello? Someone in the house? Polly?" Sam's voice came from the kitchen.

Polly fumbled with the phone.

Before she could answer it, three exuberant voices called out from upstairs, "Miss Bennett! Miss Bennett! If you're still here, don't go. We still want you to read *No, No, Donut* to us."

Sam and Essie, the girls and the dog who had come to represent so much. Polly felt pressed in on all sides and so she did the very thing she had tried too hard to convince herself she wouldn't do. She gave Donut's leash a yank and hurried out the door.

Even as she dashed down the porch steps, she hit the answer button on her phone and whispered to her sister, "Can't talk now. I'm running away."

"Polly?" Sam stepped out from the kitchen where he'd been cleaning up the water dish and food they had set out for the dog. He thought he heard footsteps on the front porch, but with the sound of Gina coming down from upstairs he couldn't be sure.

"Did she leave already?" Gina paused on the bottom step, her head tilted so she could hear the girls getting into their pajamas in their room above.

"I guess so." He willed himself not to chase after her, not to go to the door and call out into the evening for her. What would be the point? He took a step into the hallway, his eyes fixed on the door. "She didn't even say goodbye."

"You'll see her tomorrow when you take the kids to school." Gina gave a wave of her hand. "Don't *you* run off. After the girls are in bed, I want to hear this story about Polly biting you."

"She didn't bite me." He rubbed the back of his neck, choosing not to admit to his sister that while he didn't feel Polly had metaphorically chewed him out, her words had stung. He wanted to tell himself that was because they were so unfounded, but he was old enough to know that if there were no truth behind her observations, he'd have forgotten them already. "She made the mistake of saying she'd taken a bite out of me in front of Caroline and the kid took it wrong."

"Good for Polly." Gina laughed.

"You don't even know what she got onto me about," he protested.

"Did she have a point in what she said?"

Sam started to turn away, then stopped and leaned against the doorframe. "Maybe."

"I thought so." Gina laughed. "I like her, Sam. In case I haven't told you that yet. I like her a lot and anyone with eyes can see you do, too."

"Yeah, well, we all liked that little dog, too, but that isn't going to keep its real owner from coming along and taking him away." His gaze went to the bowls he'd just washed, deciding he'd take them out into the garage so they wouldn't be in the kitchen as a reminder of the times the real-life Donut—and Miss Polly Bennett—had been a part of their lives. "I don't know how I'm going to comfort the girls if that happens."

"If I know you, you'll do it the way you always do things." She turned and headed back upstairs.

"Probably." Sam rubbed his face and wished he felt better about that realization. "I guess we'll find out when the time comes."

Chapter Fourteen

Polly remained closed up in her classroom long after school had let out that next day. She used the quiet time alone, even with the rest of the school still bustling with after-school programs, to put together a montage of drawings and photos the children in her class had chosen as their best using the green-screen technology she had been working on the first day she brought Donut to school. She had brought him again today, having run home after the kids had gone to get him and bring him here to wait to hear from Ted Perry's neighbor. She raised her head to watch him sleeping in the corner of the room and a tightness gripped her throat.

He raised his head and she smiled at him but decided not to coo over him as she might have done a day ago. The letting go had to begin sometime and if she didn't make too big a fuss, it would all go smoother, right?

She focused on the task at hand, matching children's photos with the artwork they had given to her today for the class theme, "I Can." She stopped at Caroline's. "I can illustrate the book *No, No, Donut*."

Polly swept her fingertips over a drawing of a short-legged golden-brown dog with big brown eyes and long, floppy ears that appeared on her screen. It was not the only picture Caroline had done but it was her best. Polly contemplated not using it, though, what with Donut, that is, Grover, going away and Sam's feelings about the whole dog thing.

Her finger hovered over the button to click through to the next image when a small tapping on her classroom door made her jump. "Oh! Um, yes?"

Sam stuck his head in the door. "Hey! Where'd you disappear to yesterday?"

"You came all the way to the school at…" She glanced at the clock and realized it was after five. Ted Perry's neighbor would be here any minute. She clicked to reduce the image on her computer and bring up the screen saver. "…after work, to ask me that?"

Sam stepped fully into the room, chuckling.

Donut hopped up and ran over to him, tail wagging.

Polly tried to be more reserved, even though inside she was so happy he had showed up in the nick of time to be with her when she had to turn over the animal she had come to care about.

"Not exactly." Sam squatted down to scratch behind the dog's ears as he looked up at Polly and grinned. "The Go-Getters are having a rehearsal in the gym for the square-dance routine they're doing for Parents' Night next week."

Polly pushed back her chair and stood. Her knees wobbled slightly. Was that nerves over turning over Donut or a reaction to having Sam show up when she needed him and looking so handsome and happy doing it? She smoothed down her skirt and adjusted her collar. "How's that going? Caroline and the square dancing?"

"She sort of has the square part. The dancing?" He stood and gave an exaggerated wince. "I'm not ready to call what she's doing that but she'll get it. She just needs to..."

"Push herself?"

"I was going to say learn her left foot from her right." He put his hands on his hips and cocked his head. "But your way works, too."

"Actually, that's *your* way, Sam." Her low heels clacked softly on the tiled floor as she crossed the room to him. "I hesitate to ask you this, but—"

"But you're going to ask it, anyway."

She couldn't help giving him the slightest smile at calling her out on that. "Is that your way of telling me to mind my own beeswax?"

"No. No, not at all." He laughed out loud. "It might surprise you—it sure surprises me—I kind of like having someone around to meddle in my 'beeswax' about the girls. It's been a long time since I've had an objective opinion about them."

Objective. Polly knew exactly what he meant by that—outsider. Having met Max and Gina, seen him at work and heard the way people talked about him, Polly knew he had plenty of opinions handy about how he raised his daughters. Everyone had had plenty of time to form those opinions. Hers differed because she wasn't one of them. "So, about yesterday, what I said to you about... We're okay?"

"We're okay." He nodded.

She expected him to say something more, to admit her thoughts on Caroline had some validity or even dismiss it outright as having been completely forgotten.

He just kept petting Donut.

"Okay, well, maybe we could go down to the gym and take a look at how Caroline is doing?" Suddenly her own classroom felt closed in. She shifted her weight, looked down at Donut, who watched them contently, and her heart ached. "Objectively, of course."

She directed the dog to go back to his bed, jotted down a note for Ted Perry's neighbor and taped it on the window of her room before she opened the door. She and Sam stepped out into the hallway only to find Hayley and Juliette sitting on the floor with schoolbooks in their laps.

Polly's gait slowed. She could hardly swallow. She hadn't imagined that the Goodacre girls might be there to witness her surrendering Donut for good. She turned to him and in a voice hushed and constricted she said, "You didn't tell me the other girls were here."

"Homework," he said as they walked up to where the girls were waiting. "It's not just for home anymore."

"Homework? I didn't think we were assigning a whole lot of that in second grade."

"Oh, it's not a whole lot. Not unless you don't do it and let it build up." He gave Juliette and Hayley a stern look. "Neither of them have done their Parents' Night projects."

"I'm supposed to do a collage of what we hope to learn this year," Juliette said. She flipped through a magazine in her lap and tore out a page, flopping over with her hand on Hayley's shoulder as if the minimal effort had worn her to a frazzle. "It's so hard. All that sitting still for cutting and pasting. It's too much."

Especially when your time is taken up with activities from dance and gymnastics classes to Pumpkin Jumps, Polly thought, though she kept her outsider opinion to herself.

"We're doing a mobile from what Miss Bradley calls 'found objects' that show our interests." Hayley scrunched her face up. "But I can't find anything."

"Oh, I'm sure you can. It should be interesting," Polly said when what she meant was *That should be easy.* Hayley had so many interests. She could gather leaves and flowers from the farm, toy farm animals— Polly could think of a dozen things right off the bat, but she held her opinion, not comfortable interjecting herself into the situation at the moment.

Sam didn't give her a chance to speak up, anyway. He had already started toward the big double doors of the gymnasium. With a single gesture he encouraged Juliette and Hayley to come along.

Polly held her breath. She had expected having a moment as they walked along to tell Sam about the neighbor. She hurried up to him and reached out to grab him by the wrist, hoping to get him to stay back.

The girls hit the doors to the gym with a whomp. Those doors went swinging open.

Polly couldn't help but stand there, mouth open at the scene of total chaos inside.

"Caroline, please, the other way. No, the *other* other way." The school's music teacher, Allison Benson, churned her arm in a small, frantic circle trying to illustrate the way she wanted the small redhead at the center of the group to spin and move. Allison did so in perfect rhythm, never missing a beat as she continued calling the dancers' moves. "Form a circle hand in hand. Turn to your partner, right and left grand."

Caroline staggered, went the wrong way, then pivoted and fell in step. Literally, fell in her steps.

"Find your partner do-si-do." Mrs. Benson valiantly pressed on.

Caroline's partner grabbed her by the elbow to help her up and ended up sitting on the floor beside her instead.

Polly cringed and bit her lower lip to keep herself from rushing in to Caroline's rescue.

"Do-si-do?" Sam gave a nod toward Caroline and the young boy sitting beside her. "Looks more like a do-si-don't to me."

"Sam!" Polly's scowl went unnoticed as Sam continued.

"Get up, Caroline. That's the key. It's okay to fall, just keep getting up again." He clapped his hands the way she had seen her father do when her brother played soccer or when her sister, Essie, had participated in a bake-off.

Without meaning to, Polly clenched her back teeth. Tension wound across her rigid shoulders like a mantle. It took every ounce of composure she had not to grab Sam by the shirtsleeve and haul him out into the hallway like a rowdy kid.

Look at yourself! She tried to get her point across in a glare. *You have two daughters who are flailing with simple school projects and another who is literally stumbling around looking for a way to please you.* Maybe Sam's way did work for him, but he needed to take a good long look at—

"Is there a Polly Bennett in here?" A sour-faced man stood in the open door of the gym reading her name from a note in his hand. He shifted his weight from one heavy work-booted foot to the other.

Polly's mouth went dry. She had spoken with the man on the phone but had hoped his gruffness was more an outgrowth of age than of attitude. She gave Sam a fleeting glance, then stepped away from the children, not wanting to include them in this exchange. "I'm Polly."

The man raised one beefy hand with a chain leash and choke collar dangling from it. "I came for the dog."

Despite having readied herself all day, Polly froze.

"No!" Hayley rushed to Polly's side.

"Miss Bennett?" Juliette was on Hayley's heels, her eyes huge, her face tipped up at the exact angle, in a mirror image of her sister's.

Caroline scrambled to her feet and darted from the cluster of square dancers to grab her father by the hand. "You're not going to let someone we don't know take Donut, are you, Daddy? Not Donut!"

Polly swallowed hard to push down her own emotional reaction and allow herself to speak calmly and evenly about how they all knew the dog's time with them would probably be brief.

"No. No, Caroline, I'm not." Sam gave his daughter a pat that deftly guided her to the side. In two strides he was at the door with his hand extended. "I'm Sam Goodacre."

"Calvin Cooper." The man seized Sam's hand and gave it a hard shake. "I came for the dog."

"You said that, but I think you came for nothing. We're not handing the dog over to you, Mr. Cooper."

Polly covered her mouth with her hand to keep from cheering out loud. For all her criticism and concerns about the way Sam handled things, Polly felt a surge of gratitude for it. Her way, giving up and retreating, certainly would never have had the same impact.

"Ain't your dog to keep." The neighbor's jowly cheeks shook slightly with the sharpness of his words.

Sam did not back down an inch. "Nor is he yours."

"Neighbor left him with me." He gave the chain and collar in his hand a shake.

Sam crossed his arms. "And you lost him and didn't really seem to make much effort to find him."

The man gave a huff that was clearly not a denial or an admission.

"Then I think we can agree that as long as you know where the dog is and know that he's safe, your neighbor won't mind." Sam put his arm around the man and turned him away from the watchful anxious gazes of Polly and the children.

"Have to take it up with him," the neighbor grumbled.

"I've already called." He gave the man's slumped back a pat that was part camaraderie, part urging him down the hallway. "Got his number from Angela Bodine, the lady who identified him as Ted's puppy."

"Did ya?" He studied Sam.

Polly's stomach felt as if it was taking more tumbles than Caroline in the square-dance routine.

"I did what I thought was right, Mr. Cooper."

No matter how this all turned out, Polly would always remember the way Sam Goodacre took charge today. Maybe one day, if she lived in Baconburg long enough, that would be the Sam story she'd tell.

Ted Perry's neighbor heaved a weary sigh. "Don't make no never mind to me but wish you'd told me before I come all the way down here for nothing."

"I'm sorry for your trouble." Another pat from Sam that was also a little bit of a push.

The man stood there for a moment sizing up Sam through squinty eyes.

Sam made a gesture with his hand as if showing the man the way to the outside door.

It felt as if no one in the whole gymnasium so much as took a breath.

"Well, all right, then. Guess it's okay. She seems a nice enough one." He gave Polly a nod. "Told that fella he didn't have no business with a dog, anyways, him being a bachelor who stays at the station for long shifts, but he said it was a chick magnet."

"Oh, really?" Sam shot Polly a look that said he thought they had an angle they could work with, with that bit of inside information. "Did he happen to say which chick he wanted to magnetize with this dog?"

"No, but how many can there be in this town that you could meet being a fireman?" The stout older man shook his head and turned to leave, muttering as he did, "I don't get the attraction, though. Walked that dog up and down the street a dozen times the two days

before he runned off and I didn't get so much as a
'howdy' from the ladies."

He shambled out.

Sam stood at the door waving and thanking him
until the older man disappeared, then he turned to the
group.

The whole room broke out into a cheer.

Mrs. Benson threw up her hands and declared they
didn't stand much chance of getting more done today
and dismissed the group.

The girls ran to Sam, throwing their arms up to hug
him.

Polly wanted to do the same, but she managed to
control the urge long enough to walk to his side and
tell the girls to go to her room to tell Donut the good
news, then turn to him and smile. "Why did you do
that? And when did you talk to Ted Perry?"

Sam didn't look directly at her. "Didn't say I talked
to him. Said I called him."

Polly gasped. "You lied?"

"Nope, I did call." He turned to her and grinned. "I
had to leave a message, but I called. The man knows
his dog is in good hands."

"Nothing does get in your way, does it?"

"Is that a good thing or a bad one?"

"Yes." She answered looking him straight in the eye
as she moved past him, heading back to her classroom.

"What does that mean? Polly? Polly, what does
that…" He took a few steps after her and there they
were, in the hallway, alone together. He reached out
to snag her by the arm. "If you have something to say
to me, Polly, just say it."

"Just say it? Really? That's what you want? And you'll listen this time?"

He opened his mouth to say…something…but he didn't have a chance to form a thought much less a word before she grabbed his sleeve right back and gave a jerk. In three quick steps they were outside a door marked Supplies.

Polly paused to look up and down the empty hallway.

Sam followed suit, but before he could turn his head a second time, the door creaked open and she slipped inside the eight-by-five-foot walk-in closet.

Naturally, Sam didn't see any reason not to do the same.

The door shut with a bang.

She turned toward him, her lips pressed closed and her eyes flashing.

Emotions that he couldn't quite nail down played through her expressions and posture. Aggravation? Agitation? Appreciation? Maybe a little attraction, even? It didn't matter—just standing here so close to Polly with not another soul around made Sam content. And a little bit crazy. But mostly content.

"First, thank you. Thank you very much for stepping in and taking charge with Mr. Cooper. I am making myself accept that Donut will probably have to go back to his original owner, but I hated the idea of leaving him with the person who had let the little guy run away, then concluded it was for the best to leave him lost."

Yes. *Content.* In the years since Marie's death he had been resigned, accepting, motivated and even happy, but this was a feeling that he didn't think he would ever feel again. And here it was wrapped up in the guise of a dark-haired schoolteacher with a big heart and no small habit of butting into his "beeswax," as she'd put it, where his daughters were concerned. He looked deep into her eyes and smiled what he had to assume was the biggest, goofiest smile he'd smiled in a very long while.

"You're welcome," he said.

"Well, don't be too quick to think that settles everything because, you know, you *did* ask what I thought." She tipped her chin up and folded her arms, which meant she had to brush against him in the contained space.

"And I gather you think I'm just a shade shy of perfection, right, Miss Bennett?" He folded his arms, too, which had the effect of ever so slightly pushing her back and at the same time pressing their forearms against each other.

She looked down where the fabric of his rolled-back shirtsleeves met the lightly tanned skin of her bare arms. For a moment she seemed to lose her train of thought.

Sam smiled at the idea that just by being close to her he could derail her, if only for a few fleeting seconds. Somehow that seemed to make things a little more balanced out because she had completely knocked him for a loop ever since…well, since he first laid eyes on her, if he was perfectly honest with himself.

"Well, I…" She inched backward until she bumped against a shelf piled with cleaning supplies.

A bottle wobbled.

"And you wonder if I realize that this almost-imperceptible imperfection on my part keeps me from seeing that all three of my girls are struggling just a wee bit with their Parents' Night projects."

"I don't know that I'd have said—"

"Imperfection? It's all right, I'm a grown-up who can handle the criticism." Mostly by beating her to the punch with humor, he added in his mind. It was a technique he had practiced many times in the years since Marie had first gotten sick—redirect if you must, but remain in control. "Look, all kidding side, Polly, it's a new school year. There are bound to be bumps. You've probably had a few yourself already."

"I pulled you in here to talk about the girls, Sam, not about me."

"I understand your concerns. Don't worry, I've got this." He opened the door and stood back, allowing her to go out first.

He followed and let the door shut with such a wham that three other doors in the hallway swung open—and two teachers and three little girls all peeked out into the hall at them.

Don't get any big ideas. The rule still applies. No matchmaking. If the teachers hadn't been in the mix, Sam would have been tempted to shout out that warning. Instead he managed a smile and the truth, acknowledging that it sounded really weak. "Parent-teacher conference. No big deal."

"Are we in trouble?" Hayley wanted to know as Sam and Polly came toward the open door of Polly's classroom.

"No, but Miss Bennett has some very, um, legitimate worries that not one of you three is on top of your Parents' Night projects. We need to do—"

His cell phone ringing cut him off. He reached for it, explaining, "Got to take this. I'm pretty much always on call because of the pharmacy."

Polly nodded and herded the kids inside, calling out to Donut in a sweet, upbeat tone that churned up that unexpected contented feeling in Sam all over again. "Who's my good boy? Who's my pal?"

"The guy who just saved the day and let you keep your dog a little longer." Sam murmured the answer he secretly hoped was running through her head as he withdrew his phone and pressed the answer button. "Goodacre, how can I help you?"

"Yeah, Sam Goodacre? The one who left me a message?"

Sam tensed. "Could be. What was the message about?"

"My dog. I'm Ted Perry and I think you've got him."

Sam held back as the rest went inside the classroom. "Yeah, that's me. What can I do for you?"

Sam tried his best. He explained the situation about Polly being new in town, all she had done to care for the animal and even played the "owning a dog when you work long hours just for a chick magnet isn't really a great idea" card. That was one play too many.

At the mention of the potential for the dog to impress a girl, Ted turned to stone. Totally unhearing, unsympathetic, immovable stone. Sam couldn't really argue his way around a guy willing to try anything to score points with a girl. Getting a dog and leaving it with a negligent neighbor hardly made for the fuzzy-wuzzy feelings in women. The best the guy would agree to was to let Polly visit when she wanted. Other than that, the guy wanted his dog back and he wanted him back in two days.

So much for near perfection. Sam rubbed his hand over his face and groaned. He should never have gotten mixed up in all this. He should have stuck with his plan from the very beginning. He should have done things the way he always did.

His girls were floundering because he hadn't pushed them enough. Time to fix that. The only way to do that was to take control. Sam knew just how to do that, but he might have to break one of his rules to get it done. Hey, as long as he was the one doing the rule-breaking, right?

Sam didn't allow himself a chance to rethink the question. He grabbed the door handle and came strolling into Polly's classroom with his head high. "I've been thinking. Because Grover already has an owner and everyone here really seems to have caught a bad case of puppy love…"

The girls giggled at the phrase.

Polly's back went stiff, her eyes guarded.

Sam slapped his hands together in a thunderous clap and even as everyone jumped he announced his new plan louder still. "So, how about this? If you girls buckle down and get everything done to show well at Parents' Night on Friday, I will be willing to reconsider *one* of my rules."

"You're going to date Miss Bennett?" Juliette leaped up.

"No!" Sam held up his hands. Pressing on without

daring to look Polly's way after the definitiveness of his response, he kept his focus strictly on the girls and said, "I'm going to look into us getting our own dog."

Chapter Fifteen

"A dog? He promised those children a dog if they came through with their Parents' Night projects?" Essie's disbelief about Sam's rash decision came out clearly through the phone, then was softened by a laugh. "Did he not think about the implications of breaking his own rules?"

"Well, that's the deal with him, I think." Polly had started off the very conversation with her twin with the incredible news of Sam's announcement. He had been so proud of his solution, but now, three days and one returned dog later, Polly still couldn't quite believe it. "It was so obvious that he wanted to make everyone feel better about the situation. Wanted it badly enough to do this. He *makes* the rules, so he's just making a new one. That's okay with him as long as he sees it as progress."

"I can see that."

"I thought you would. Go, go, go. Win, win, win," Polly said like a cheer, knowing her sister would revel in it, not take it as criticism.

With Parents' Night at Van Buren Elementary only

an hour away, Polly used the call to try to calm her nerves as she dressed for the event. She put the phone on speaker so she could contort herself to try to zip up the yellow dress she'd chosen because it looked so cheerful and also because it wouldn't show any left-over dog hair.

In the background of the call Polly heard an electronic ding and a car door slam. She gave up with the zipper still halfway open. "Speaking of going, tell me you are not going to drive and talk on the phone at the same time. I know you're busy, but—"

"I have Bluetooth, but rest assured I am not driving and talking on the phone anymore."

The doorbell rang.

Polly jumped. Her mind filled with images of Ted Perry returning her dog or Sam showing up with a puppy, even as she told herself that would never happen.

"Hold on, someone's at the door." She hurried through the living room and peered out the small window to see who was on her front porch. "Essie!"

In a second she'd clicked off the phone, swung open the door and had her arms around her twin. The two laughed and hugged and chattered so quickly that no one else would have been able to keep up.

"Why? How?" Polly asked, guiding Essie inside, overnight case in tow. "Don't you have to work?"

"I deserve a weekend off now and then." Essie spun Polly away, zipped up the dress, then spun her back.

"Now and then? Meaning once in a blue moon?" Polly double-checked to make sure the top of the zipper got buttoned down. "You never take time off."

"I do when my sister needs me. After that phone call saying you were running away and the email saying how happy you were that Donut had been reunited with his very, very, very nice owner, what else could I do?"

"Was it that obvious I'm miserable?" Polly started to search for her shoes.

Essie didn't even ask what Polly was looking for, just bent to peer under the couch, nabbed them and handed them to Polly. "The last 'very' did it."

She slid her feet into the practical but pretty flats, then headed off for the kitchen to grab her purse. "Ted Perry is a nice guy."

"I'm sure he is but he's not the guy I want to know about." Essie followed along and had hardly gotten through the kitchen door when she plucked up Sam's hat. When she brandished it, she didn't need words to warn Polly that she had her all figured out.

"I keep meaning to find a way to have that fixed." Polly sighed. "Though I'm almost convinced he doesn't really want it back. It's all about this moving-forward idea of his. He thinks it is progress. I think it's a way not to deal with the pain of his loss."

"Some things you can't fix, Polly. This hat is only one of them. A grown man who has made up his mind about how he wants to live his life and raise his kids is another."

"But those girls need some balance in their lives." Polly reached out and took the hat from Essie's hand. "And Sam? Sam looked good in this hat. Though I have thought he'd look better in this smoky-brown trilby with a black band that I found online."

Essie laughed and stood up. Smack off a ten-plus-hour drive, she looked fresh and ready to go without doing anything more than whisking her hand down her navy blue skirt and then over her slicked-back black hair. "In other words, it's too soon for you to give up on them."

Polly had never thought of it that way. For all her big ideas about slowing down the pace of life and taking things as they came, did Polly have her own drive to succeed, to try to make things turn out "her" way?

It was with that question in her mind and a jumble of emotions—sadness over Donut, anxiety about the girls' big night tonight, joy at seeing Essie and conflict over whether to tell her twin there was dog hair on her blue skirt, mingled in with her tender feelings about Sam—pinging around inside her, Polly and Essie headed for school and Parents' Night.

"Mrs. Williams says my collage is super-creative, Daddy."

"It's not all pictures of dogs, is it?" Sam teased Juliette as he stood by the open side door as the girls climbed out.

"Not *all* of it," she shot back with a sly smile. "Just one, I think."

"You *think?*" He watched her lead the parade of redheads into the school building. "Girls, wait!"

"We can't wait, Daddy, we have to go-o-o," Juliette called as they hurried along the hallway.

The threesome reached the little girls' room and Hayley turned around and waved him away. "Go get us a seat in the bleachers. A *good* seat."

Caroline added, "Don't wait for us, Dad. We're not babies."

"I guess they told you." Polly came out of the restroom brushing dog hair from her dark skirt, wearing a smug smile and her usually untamable hair in a tight ponytail at the back of her head.

He started to say something, but nothing came readily to his lips. He knew she was still smarting from having to hand over the little lost dog, but it was not in him to dredge up pain or loss that belonged in the past.

It didn't matter because Polly didn't linger long enough to chat. She gave a wave and headed off to her classroom.

That made sense, of course, because parents were already arriving, although he couldn't contain a subtle grin when he spotted her peering in at the doorway a little bit later during the Go-Getters square dancing routine.

Mrs. Benson took her position and called to the children to get their "sets in order" and they all took their places. Sam stole a peek at Polly only to find she had whipped out a cell phone, clearly to record the event.

The song began and he could hear Juliette and Hayley cheer her on, but he admittedly missed some of Caroline's performance. Partly because he wasn't sure he wanted to see it, missteps and all. But also partly because he kept glancing Polly's way hoping to catch her delighting at Caroline's willingness to stick with it no matter what.

Juliette gasped.

Hayley giggled.

Sam whipped his head around to see Caroline falter, overcorrect and start out doing an allemande left in the wrong direction, then give a twirl and correct herself.

"That a girl." Sam beamed with pride in Polly's direction only to find she had left.

When the music stopped, Sam was the first on his feet applauding, which seemed to embarrass Caroline and then Juliette and Hayley rather than impress them. For all his talk of pushing them ahead, in that moment it dawned on him that they were growing up so fast.

He leaned down to Hayley, who had been sitting next to him, and asked above the shuffling of children as the Go-Getters left and the next group of performers came onto the floor. "I don't suppose you girls want to take me to your classrooms to see your projects now, do you?"

The two exchanged looks, then searched to find Caroline in the crowd. Hayley put her hand on his leg and gave him a nudge away from them. "You go on, Daddy. We'll stay and watch the next group."

He didn't wait around to be told twice. Of course, he started with Caroline's teacher first. "Hey, saw you got the big square-dance number on your phone."

"I, uh, yes." Polly's ponytail bounced as she looked around the large metal cart where she'd been adjusting the feeds hooked to a big television set. A slide show of smiling faces and school projects faded in and out accompanied by a hit-or-miss audio track. "Look, I think you should know—"

"You don't have to apologize." He held up his hand.

"It worked out well for the girls and that's what matters."

"Apologize?" She stood straight and narrowed her eyes at him in a way he'd never seen her do before. She shook her head and pointed her finger at him in a way that felt like if he'd been closer, she'd have jabbed him in the shoulder as she spoke. "Oh, I get it. You're talking about that entirely ill-conceived 'win a pet for your performance' deal you made with your daughters, aren't you?"

"Ill-conceived? Win a pet? Polly, that doesn't sound like you."

"Because it's not me." Black hair barely contained by a headband, Polly stood up from behind the over-size TV cart.

"There's—" Sam looked from one to the other "—there's two of you?"

Polly came and stood beside her carbon copy. "Sam Goodacre, meet my sister, Esther Bennett. Essie, meet Sam."

"You're…"

"Identical," they both said at the same time.

"But only one of us has a reason to ask you what on earth you think I would have to apologize to you for." Polly crossed her arms and met his gaze in that spitfire-with-a-cause way of hers.

Immediately he knew he'd never consider them identical again. Amusement met the sense of contentment Polly seemed to always awaken in him. How could he have ever thought this stiff-backed, slick-haired, neatly contained woman was his Polly? *His* Polly! The thought threw him off-balance for a second.

That was long enough for Polly to swoop across the room and have him by the shirtsleeve. She was all fire and feistiness as she opened her mouth and said, "Now, listen to me, Sam Goodacre, I—"

"I like it when you grab my shirtsleeve," he murmured.

"W-well, you're not going to like what I—" she glanced down at the place where her hand held the soft blue fabric of his shirt "—have to say."

"Never mind me." Polly's twin all but disappeared behind the TV as she called out, "I'll keep on working to get this sound synced up and running."

"Maybe I won't like it, but I'm so glad you're talking to me that right now I'm happy to hear you out."

She blinked her big eyes as if she couldn't quite remember what she intended to say. Then she shook her head, pressed her lips together and gave his sleeve a shake. "That's a sweet thing to say, but I'm not talking to you as a friend right now. Well, not as *just* a friend. I have to tell you this."

He shifted his feet as if bracing himself for some big news when really he just wanted to move a little closer to her. "Yeah, I know. You don't think much more of my promising the girls a dog than your sister does."

"Actually, I don't really know what to think about getting the girls a dog, but I do have something to tell you about what they have done to live up to your demands."

"Demands?" He stepped back at that.

She stepped forward after him. "Sam, I think the girls have been running the oldest game in the identicals' playbook. The old switcheroo."

"The old… Polly, are you saying Caroline, Juliette and Hayley have been trading places?"

"Trading places is just one part of it. Sam, I haven't confirmed it with Mrs. Williams and Mrs. Bradley yet because I wanted to talk to you about it first, but I think Caroline may have done some of Hayley's and Juliette's work while Juliette did the square dance in Caroline's place."

He pulled his arm away, freeing his sleeve, trying to laugh off the notion. "How could you say that? Polly, you weren't even there."

"That's one reason I can say it." She went over and shut the door, the accepted signal that a parent and teacher were talking and to wait until they were done to come inside. "When I watched the replay of it on Essie's phone—"

"You sent your sister to spy on my kids?"

"No! No, Sam, she went down while I was setting up here. I asked her to record it because I wanted to see the performance. Because—"

He tried to make sense of it all and in doing so could only come to two conclusions. Either he was all wrong about the way he'd handled the girls or—

An image flashed on the screen behind Polly.

"You think you know better than me what's right for my kids," he said, his jaw tight.

"No, Sam, I never said that."

"You don't have to say it. I'm looking at the proof of it right now." He pointed to the image of Caroline in front of a drawing of a dog that Sam recognized instantly as Donut. "Why would you let her draw a picture of a dog she could never have, then choose it to show at Parents' Night?"

"I don't tell the kids what to draw or write about, Sam. The project was to write a poem, story or do a piece of art with the topic 'I Can,' and that's what Caroline drew."

"Donut, Polly? 'I can have Donut as my dog'?" His gut twisted, not from anger but a kind of helpless emptiness that he hadn't felt in a long time. He had worked every day since Marie had gotten sick to keep the girls from dwelling on how fragile relationships could be, how quickly someone we love could be lost and now— "Why would you do that to a little girl who had already had so much sadness in life, Polly?"

"No, you have to hear the audio that goes with it."

"I think I've heard enough." He turned to leave, his head so clouded with a whirlwind of thoughts that he didn't trust what he might say if he stayed. "I have to get going."

"So that's how you're going to handle this?" Polly hurried to place herself between Sam and the door. "Like you do everything. Sam's way. Just charge straight ahead, no looking back, no time to stop and consider if you're headed in the right direction?"

"Step aside, Polly." He did not meet her gaze this time. "The girls are in the gym. I need to get them and meet with their other teachers."

"I know loss is painful. Even for people of faith it's hard to understand how a loving God would take away someone we love, especially when we still need them so much. But plunging blindly forward isn't the way to get past that. Some things take time."

"Don't lecture me. Don't you lecture me, Polly Bennett." She wouldn't let him go, wouldn't let him do what he thought was best—keep moving. Sam felt hurt and embarrassed at that hurting. He was angry, but not sure why he was angry. His head throbbed and his heart ached, and when Polly wouldn't get out of his way physically, he did the only thing he knew how to do. Plowed right over her, verbally. "You've come running home to a place mostly made up in your imagination to keep from dealing with the fact that life never measured up to your expectations. You accuse me of running from the past. Well, you've run *to* the past and what has that gotten you?"

His harsh words worked, too. Polly stepped back and let him go.

He couldn't just let it go at that, though. "I do not think my girls would do that, and even if they did, don't you think I'd know it?"

"Yes, I do think you would if you weren't so fixated on them being the best and always having to come out on top of whatever they tackle." Polly's words rushed out and her voice went a notch higher with the power of her emotional connection to what she wanted to express. "A family should support each other, not compete, not try to have to win approval of their parent with every endeavor."

"Whoa, I never said they had to be the best at anything." He held up his hand to stop her right there. "I know you think Caroline is doing all this to make me happy, Polly, but the rest of this... I don't think that's about me at all."

Esther Bennett popped up from behind the cart, her

eyes wide and her mouth open. After she got Polly's attention, she folded her arms and tipped her head to one side.

Sam didn't have to be the father of multiples to recognize the silent communication between the two. And
suddenly a few other things became clear to him.

"Polly, this is *my* family. I know yours had problems and you wish things had been different but you
can't fix your past here." He spread his arms wide to
indicate the classroom and, in a larger sense, all of the
town she had come to in search of a new life. "You
have to come to terms with it and move on, find something better, make it better. That's how you heal."

"Have you done that, Sam? Come to terms with
losing Marie?" Polly never took her eyes from his despite her sister's looming presence and the muffled
voices from the hallway outside. "You've moved on,
you've tried and tried and tried to find something
better, but has any of that made your life better?"

Sam honestly could not answer that, so instead he
crossed to the door and opened it, saying quietly, "I
told you my rules, Polly. I never lied to you or pretended to be anything or anyone but who I am. I wish
you had honored that."

"I did honor it, Sam," she called after him. "I honored it by being your friend and telling the truth when
nobody else would. You can't keep running forever.
At some point you need to slow down and take a good
hard look at what's going on around you. Maybe then
you'd see that I am on your side."

Polly's words stayed with Sam the rest of the evening. So much so that he found himself arguing against

them when he should have been paying attention to the tour of Juliette's and Hayley's classrooms. Neither of those teachers even hinted at anything amiss with the girls' work, though. That proved Sam was in the right here, right?

Sam was still wrestling with all of it when he and the girls got home. Max leaned back in his chair at the kitchen table and hollered out as the girls ran upstairs. "So do we need to build a doghouse or not?"

"Yeah." Gina, who had met them on the porch and, true to the small-town grapevine, had already heard that Polly and Sam had had words, prodded Sam through the doorway. She pushed past him to tell their younger sibling, "By all means, build a dog house— then we can send Sam to it."

"Me? *Why me?*" Sam knew why. At the very least his behavior on this night meant to let the children show off was in bad form. "Polly's the one who accused the girls of pulling the old switcheroo. I was just defending my daughters."

Gina glared at him. "I think what you were defending was your own wounded ego."

Sam clenched his jaw. "She was trying to—"

"She was trying to be a good teacher, Sam, *and* a good friend."

"Whoa, switcheroo? Defending what?" Max stood and gestured broadly as he spoke. "Clue a guy in, will ya?"

"There's nothing to clue you in on." Sam pivoted on his boot heel and headed for the hallway. He didn't have to take this in his own home. He was Sam Good-

acre. He had a plan. He had a way of doing things that
always worked for him. No stopping, no looking back.

Except…he twisted his head to glance over his
shoulder at the door just as headlights slashed across
the front of the old farmhouse.

"Who's that?" Gina rushed into the hall. "Do you
think something's wrong?"

Sam ignored his sister's question as he headed for
the door, flung it open and stepped out into the September night air to greet the woman he knew he'd find
coming up the walk.

Chapter Sixteen

"I saw Caroline mess up in the routine." Sam came out of the house on the defense but not sounding like a man fully convinced of what he was saying. "If Juliette had been doing it, she would have gotten through it without a hitch."

"Not if she didn't have a chance to rehearse it," Polly called out as she climbed from her car.

Sam slowed his pace.

Polly's already-rapid heartbeat kicked up into at least double-time. She leaned in to look at Essie in the passenger seat and said, "Are you sure this is a good idea?"

"Hey, you know me, I'd never suggest anything half-baked." Essie waved to her to go ahead to talk to Sam. Then she put her hand on the door handle. "If you need me, I'll be here for you."

"Will you?" Polly asked sincerely. "Because it seems to me you've been mostly somewhere else, Essie. Always ahead of me. Always putting in a few more hours of work to stay ahead of everyone."

"If you felt that way…" Essie caught herself. "Why am I saying 'if'?"

Essie's eyes met Polly's. "I know I've bought into the whole 'do more, be more' attitude of Mom and Dad. And I know what it did to you, Polly."

"If it helps, in watching Sam and his girls, I'm beginning to see what it did to *you,* too, Essie."

"I guess we both need to deal with the pressures of our past, huh? That's what you were doing by becoming a teacher and moving here. I can't tell you how much I admire you for it."

"Really?" Tears welled in Polly's eyes. "For once, maybe you could follow my lead."

"I'll take that under consideration."

On the drive out here they had had a long-overdue heart-to-heart where Polly unloaded her feelings of never measuring up. Essie had laughed at that, not to be dismissive but because she had always felt that Polly was the one who had everything figured out, not bowing to their parents' need to push the family so hard as evidence the divorce hadn't left lasting scars.

Their parents had meant well; they wanted to make the best out of a lousy situation, the twins had concluded. Just as Sam was trying to do with his girls.

In seeing her own folks as loving and wanting so badly to do the right thing for their children as Sam, even if they didn't go about it in the best way, Polly began to view things differently. That led her straight out to the Goodacre family farmhouse.

"You saw a redheaded girl with her hair in a ponytail like Juliette's instead of Caroline's pigtails make a mistake and recover from it without causing so much as a stumble." Polly shut the car door and turned to Sam. She kept her tone even, reasoned and, some might say, loving. "Isn't that just what someone might do if they had a handful of gymnastics programs and dance recitals under their belt?"

Sam stopped. He was halfway between the house and Polly's car. "Polly, you're saying you honestly want me to believe my girls…my Sunday school–going, raised-to-know-right-from-wrong girls pulled off this elaborate switch? That they'd lie, in essence, to fool their teachers and cheat me into giving them a dog of their own?"

"I don't think they thought they were lying, Sam." She came to him. There in the quiet of the darkening September sky she moved in until she stood so close that she only had to tip her head back slightly to look up into his kind, searching-for-understanding eyes. "I think…I *know* in my heart…they thought they were *helping* each other and helping *you*."

His brow furrowed. He did not look directly into her gaze. "Helping *me?*"

"Making you happy, Sam." She took a deep breath and held it a second, thought of all the years of keeping her true feelings to herself and what that had cost her, then reached out and slipped her hand in his. "They got a clear message that doing all these things and doing them well—following your rules—was what it would take to make you happy."

"But I made the rules to try to make them happy," he said softly. He raised his head and looked into her eyes. "Honest, Polly, that's all I ever wanted."

"That's all you *think* you wanted, Sam. But happy

wasn't really your primary concern after Marie died, was it?"

He looked toward the front door, then up at the light shining from the second-story bedroom of the three little girls. At last he looked at Polly, then bowed his head slightly and gave it a slow shake. "No, I wanted to protect them from all the pain I was going through."

"You accused me of running away to a dream that never existed, Sam."

"Polly, I—"

"No, you were right. My own family said pretty much the same thing." Polly held her free hand up, then brought it down to join her other hand on top of his. "They were right and they were wrong. Maybe I did run to an overly romanticized, even imaginary, past, but I arrived in Baconburg, met you and came home."

He looked at her hands around his, then at her.

Her heart rate slowed. Her breathing, which she just realized had been quick and shallow, eased. Looking into Sam's eyes now she knew he hadn't just heard what she'd said, he had listened. She really did feel now that the things she had dreamed of were possible—family, home, even love someday.

Sam's shoulders rose and fell, then he took both her hands in his, turning them over as if studying them to see how she had done this trick of getting right to the heart of the matter. "I don't see how this changes anything, Polly. I still want to protect my girls. I still want to teach them the skills I think they need to cope with all that can go wrong in life."

She heard his words, but she had to ask, to clarify his meaning. "And I am something that can go wrong?"

He looked at her and said nothing.

The night seemed to close in around them. The light of the Goodacre home over Sam's shoulders now made it seem distant and unreachable.

"I see." She tried not to burst into tears right there on the spot.

Sam stood there talking about teaching his children his way to deal with the pain of loss. Wasn't that just what she had done coming here? Full speed ahead without looking back? She thought about warning him, once again, that his way did not work for everyone.

It sure hadn't worked for her. So she relied on what worked for her. She turned to leave. "I hope I *am* wrong, Sam, about the girls and the switcheroo."

"Polly, I didn't mean for things to turn out like this," he called after her."

"Neither did I." She reached her car.

"I'm sure I'll see you around," he said, as if a neighborly shout-out would somehow move them quickly and smoothly into the next phase of their relationship. "It's a small town, after all."

She turned and looked at him standing there framed by his home, his life still every bit intact as it was the day they met. She made a mental photo, one more moment frozen in time of someone who would no longer be in her life. "It could be a whole city of strangers, Sam, the way I feel right now."

He stepped toward her.

She shook her head to tell him not to bother. He didn't want her to interfere in his life or the lives of his children unless she did things his way. Trying to make the man happy was a waste of time. He didn't want to be happy. He wanted to be in control.

There were some things she couldn't fix, couldn't teach and now, couldn't run away from. If that was the only lesson she learned from all of this, Polly decided that would be enough for a long time to come.

Three little girls with red hair in curls.

Sam peeked in to see the triplets all sitting on the same bed, talking with their heads pressed together.

He tapped on the doorframe before he stepped across the threshold of the open door. "Prayer time, girls?"

They scrambled to their own beds and knelt beside them.

Sam's stomach knotted. He didn't want to think his children could have played this trick on him and the teachers, but even more than that, that they could kneel and say their prayers in front of him knowing they'd done it. It didn't sit right with him. He straightened up. "You know, girls, before we start prayers, maybe we should take a minute to talk."

The three exchanged glances.

"About what?" Hayley, the bold, asked without exactly meeting her dad's eyes.

"Well, for starters, I don't want there ever to be secrets between us." As soon as he said it, Sam wished he hadn't. He thought of Polly, the kiss they had shared. Then of his attempts to get Ted Perry to hand over Donut while still adhering to his no-dogs rule for the girls. "That doesn't count for the things that are just for adults. Things that I'm not ready to share with you."

They definitely looked confused.

Last he thought of the argument he'd had with Polly tonight at the school and her saying she suspected they'd pulled "the old switcheroo." Sam had to know that news of him and Polly clashing was probably already making the rounds. He could just imagine someone in his girls' Sunday school overhearing the story even now.

"But then there are things that happen out in the open, things other people in town might be talking about." He fumbled to find the right way to tell just the part they needed to hear.

All three faces tipped up in unison and at the same angle. In the dim light even their expressions seemed exactly the same. Sam had to concede that under the right circumstances even he could have been duped into believing Juliette was Caroline in the gymnasium this evening.

He crossed to the three desks where the girls usually did their homework, trying to give them time to unburden themselves if they had gotten up to any funny business to cash in on his Parents' Night promise. He leaned in to peer more closely at stacks of paper and extra clippings left over from the collage still hanging in Juliette's classroom. On one hand it did not seem likely that Juliette sat still and cut neatly around each picture pasted onto white foam board. He surveyed the desk with pink pens and stickers and even a small bottle of pink glitter on the corner. On the other hand, he had no proof she didn't.

He turned and some chicken feathers dangling by bright green yarn tied to a small tree limb smacked him along the side of the face. He turned and blew a wayward feather from in front of his nose. He thought the girls would giggle at him tangled up in Hayley's mobile, but instead they grew strangely quiet.

He thought of the day at the drugstore when the threesome had tried unsuccessfully to fool Polly and how Caroline had cracked and confessed everything so quickly. He'd certainly had the impulse to lay everything out in the open about his words with Polly when he'd seen their faces.

The fact that they didn't say a thing made him think maybe he was right about the girls. They just sat there listening to him, seemingly in no hurry to talk to him about anything, anything at—

"Wait a minute. What's up here?" Sam spun around and once again the chicken feathers went dancing on their green yarn tethers. "I have been in this room three whole minutes and not a one of you has asked when we're getting that dog I promised."

Three worried looks.

"We don't want any dog but Donut, Daddy," Caroline finally said softly. The other girls nodded almost simultaneously.

Sam's heart sank. All this. He had broken his rule, asked his girls to give the proverbial one-hundred-and-ten-percent, gone to Parents' Night and not even taken the time to properly appreciate or even look at their handiwork. And for what?

They didn't want any dog but Donut.

Polly didn't want anything but what was best for his girls.

Sam didn't want anything but for his life to go back to the way it was when he was in charge of it all and nothing held him back.

He groaned and rubbed his eyes, then motioned for the girls to get to their own beds and say their prayers. As they knelt down to begin, Sam slipped into the hallway, not sure he could stand by and hear those three sweet kids ask for God to bless the dog they couldn't have and the woman who thought they would resort to cheating just to please him.

Sam shut his eyes to keep from allowing himself to overthink that. Polly was a good person, a *really* good person. But she did admit she'd re-created the Baconburg of her childhood into something straight out of *The Andy Griffith Show,* starring him as the kindly single dad who needed the loving guidance of the local schoolteacher. She suspected the girls of pulling this prank because it fit with her idea of how things would work out. She'd point out the problem. He'd see the error of his ways and then—

"And if our mommy is near You, tell her it's okay. We have Miss Bennett to help us down here now."

Sam jerked his head around to peer into the darkened room but not soon enough to identify which girl had said that.

Then nothing. Sam had formulated his plan with careful forethought. He had a job to do where the girls were concerned and allowing them to form attachments to a dog and now Polly were big mistakes. But mistakes that could be undone.

He just had to get the girls to really kick things up a notch. Tomorrow he'd call the mom in charge of the Go-Getters and offer to have the group hold another fundraiser at the Pumpkin Jump and maybe he'd just suggest they'd be welcome to do their square-dance routine, as well.

That's exactly what he'd do—full speed ahead.

Chapter Seventeen

The next two weeks flew by for Polly. Her pupils had settled into the school routine nicely and the other teachers informed her that fall was a crazy-busy time for the small Ohio town that relied heavily on agriculture and tourism to pay the bills through the winter. This left very little time for Polly to sit and pine for Donut or her family. But somehow she still had plenty of time to think about Sam Goodacre.

"It's that hat," Polly told Essie on a late-night phone call while Polly graded test papers over what her students had learned in the first six weeks. "I need to get it back to him."

"Or throw it away," Essie countered. "He doesn't want it."

"Then *he* can throw it away. *I* can't. Not a hat his late wife gave him." Polly set down her pen and rubbed her eyes. "Maybe I can mail it to him."

Essie laughed.

"Better yet, come up to the Pumpkin Jump on Saturday, pretend to be me and give it to him yourself."

"That sounds more like wanting to *be* right than to

do right," Essie used another of their mother's sayings to call out Polly. "It's time to stop hiding in the past, Polly. There are some things you can't fix, but you're living proof that you can start again."

"That's a nice idea, but how can you start again with someone who won't slow down long enough to notice the things around them that they *can* fix?" Polly sighed and said her goodbyes. She started to put the phone down, but as she stretched to put it far enough away that it wouldn't further distract her, the photos on the mantel came into her line of vision.

She picked up the phone again and touched the button to look through her contact list. After only a couple clicks she pulled up the pic she'd taken of Sam, Caroline and Donut on the fire truck. She tried to smile but couldn't quite pull it off.

"I was not wrong about the triplets," she told the man smiling out at her from a moment frozen in time. She pointed at his face, then gave it a poke for emphasis. "I am not hiding in the past. And I am definitely not going to the…"

"Hello? Polly? Are you okay?"

"…Pumpkin Jump," she murmured, realizing she had tapped Sam's name, placing a call to him, when she meant to tap the photo. Her heart stopped.

"You calling about the Pumpkin Jump? At this hour? Polly?"

"Hi, Sam, actually I didn't mean to call at all. Sorry." She moved her thumb to the end-call button.

"It's good to hear your voice."

She curled her hand closed and said softly, "You, too."

"I… What was that about the Pumpkin Jump?"

"I tried to get Essie to come to it, but…"

"She should. You should bring her."

"I wasn't planning to come if she doesn't, Sam, but it was good to hear your voice." She did hang up this time.

Polly thought that was that until the morning of the big event when her doorbell rang.

Even after all this time, Polly still hoped, just a little bit, that she'd find Sam holding Donut on the other side. Instead—

"Essie! You said you couldn't come for the Pumpkin Jump!" Polly threw her arms around her sister.

"I wasn't going to, but I went online to find this…" She thrust out the smoky-brown trilby Polly had admired as perfect for Sam.

Polly gasped and took it in her hands as the two of them came inside.

"And then I had to check out this Pumpkin Jump and lookie what's going on there." She held up a printout that included not just a photo of the pumpkins she and Sam and Caroline had picked out, but also a schedule of events that included a dog-wash fundraiser and a square-dance routine by the Van Buren Elementary Go-Getters.

Chaos and fun, work and worry, it all came together the morning of the Goodacre Organic Farm's Annual Pumpkin Jump. Sam actually had very little to do with the event, which meant he was the one everyone expected to be available to help them with their part. He didn't mind. He liked being able to move around the edges of the activities; it gave him a chance to see who was there.

"Nobody has seen her," Max muttered as he pushed past Sam carrying a tray piled high with hamburger buns.

Sam opened his mouth to deny he'd been looking for anyone in particular then caught a glimpse of the girls trailing along behind their uncle, each carting her own giant jar of mustard, mayo or ketchup. He grinned at them, so proud to see them pitching in like that. In fact, for the past two weeks, they had pretty much been giving every effort their all and everyone seemed very happy.

The operative word being *seemed*. A dull heaviness lay on his chest. Sam just couldn't believe that after having Polly and Donut in their lives, things could go back to normal so easily. He tried to tell himself that kids were resilient, they bounced back quickly, but if he had ever really trusted in that he would never have had to come up with even his simple set of rules.

"If we see her, we'll tell her you're looking for her," Max called back as he led the girls toward the place where he was about to fire up a huge portable grill.

"Her, who?" Hayley asked, never even looking Sam's way.

"We aren't looking for a 'her.' We're looking for a 'him,'" Juliette announced as she passed.

"Him?" News to Sam. "Him, who?"

"Donut, Daddy." Caroline paused long enough to get a better grip on the plastic jug of mustard in her arms. "The Go-Getters are having another dog wash and the firemen are helping. That means Donut is coming, right?"

Sam felt as if he'd just taken a punch in the gut. "Dog wash? I didn't plan for—"

"There are some things in life you can't plan for, Sam."

"Polly!" Without thinking over the implications, he grabbed her by the shoulders, leaned in and kissed her cheek. "Am I ever glad to see you."

The minute she was in his arms, everything felt right with the world. Or at least as if she could help him make it right.

Polly gave a nervous laugh and pushed at his chest, probably to give herself some breathing room—a stark reminder that no matter how good it felt to see her again, there was still a lot standing between them.

"Did you know about this dog-wash deal?" he asked before she could even get a word out.

She shook her head. "Not until this morning when—"

"And you just came? You weren't going to come, but you did." He grabbed her by the hand and began to walk. "We can still get this under control, but we need to go, and go fast."

"Sam?" She stumbled forward a few steps before she caught up with his pace. "Have you ever stopped to think that just because *you* aren't in control it doesn't mean things are *out of* control?"

"I've missed you, Polly." He glanced back at her and chuckled. "But we don't have time for philosophy. If the girls have Donut taken away again, I don't know what it will do to them."

"You mean what it will do to you." She twisted her arm to free her hand from his, then turned toward the stand where Max and the girls were busy setting up. "Sam, the girls look fine."

"Of course they do. They probably have some wild idea that they will be able to get Donut as the dog I promised them. It's the only dog they wanted." He scanned the field where people were arriving, then the path leading toward the barn where the doors were flung open and a local band was warming up for the performances to come. "Let's see if we can find Gina and find out where this dog wash is going to be set up."

"Or you could just go over to the big yellow fire truck." Polly pointed to an area in the open field where the truck sat surrounded by kids.

"Great." Without hesitation, Sam grabbed her arm and started out again.

"Sam!" More foot-dragging. "Did you listen to yourself? I said the kids are fine. You're trying to fix something that hasn't even happened yet."

"That's my job." He cupped her elbow and kept walking.

This time she dug in her heels and they stayed dug in enough that Sam's hand slipped and she jerked to a stop. He pivoted to face her.

Even standing in the middle of a small crush of people, amid booths being set up, hay bales and pumpkins stacked to direct people to various venues, when Sam looked Polly's way, she was all he could see. And despite all the things whirling around them, she made him smile.

"Your job? Really? I thought Sam's way was to

teach the girls that no matter what happened you could just push your way through and get on with life." She folded her arms. "I thought *that* was your job."

"You got me." He held his hands out to his side. "Where Hayley, Juliette and Caroline are concerned, I... Look, Polly, I made this impulsive promise to the girls that they could have a dog if they came through for Parents' Night and the only dog they want is Donut. So if Ted Perry shows up with that dog and leaves with him, it will be like I am the one taking him away from them. I don't think I could stand that."

"Oh, Sam." She put her hand to his cheek. "That is the first time you ever actually said it."

He leaned into her hand. "Said what?"

"The real reason why you have pushed the girls to do things your way. Because you can't stand the idea of their being hurt," she said quietly. "Sam, did you ever consider that this is about your grief, not the girls'?"

Before he'd met Polly, he'd have shot that down in a heartbeat. Now he actually stood there with her hand on his and could hear his own heart pounding in his chest, steady and strong. "I have no idea what to say to that, Polly."

"That's probably the best answer you could have given, Sam." She dropped her hand and laughed.

He opened his mouth to say more, but the sound of the fire engine's siren reverberated through the air, cutting him off.

Polly jumped forward.

He caught and steadied her by putting both hands on her arms. Their eyes met and they both broke out laughing at being taken by surprise.

"Hey, I…" Max came thundering up on them, stopped hard and leaned back, a stunned expression on his face.

Sam stepped away from Polly. Open as he was to exploring that he hadn't properly grieved for Marie and the life he and the girls had lost, he didn't want his family to get any ideas that he and Polly were suddenly fair matchmaking game.

"Look, Max, I…"

"You…" Max pointed at Polly. "You're…"

"Look, don't read anything into this." Sam waved his hand, and put his back to the fire truck and his plans to head off any potential issues with Donut and Ted Perry. "I just met Polly out here and—"

"And I just met her back there." Max jerked his thumb over his shoulder.

"Your sister?" Sam looked at Polly.

She nodded.

"And you and the girls thought you've been talking to Polly?" he asked Max.

"Well, we haven't talked to her—she was on her cell phone the whole time—but she looks like Polly and sounds like Polly and she…" Max made an overly played wince, then a slow look of realization came over his face. He started to chuckle. "The girls don't know?"

"I didn't tell them." Sam looked at Polly. "I sort of stopped their talking about you except as Caroline's teacher after…"

"This should be interesting," Max said as he turned and headed back to his booth, motioning for them to follow. "C'mon, I need your help, old man."

Max grabbed Sam by the arm and shoved him into the forefront of the three of them. Sam tried to look back to say something to Polly about how they should tell the girls about her twin but before he could, the triplets came rushing up to him, Juliette in pink, Hayley in green and Caroline…also in pink?

"Dad! Dad! Dad!" they called all together. "Miss Bennett is here, Miss Bennett…"

Hayley pulled up short. Juliette bumped into her back and Caroline into hers.

"Hi, girls!" Polly wriggled her fingers in a wave.

They looked from the real Polly to her twin.

Sam braced himself for them to break out laughing with delight to have learned that their new friend had something more in common with them. But nobody laughed.

Hayley looked at Juliette. Juliette looked at Caroline. Caroline looked at Hayley.

Sam shut his eyes as everything Polly had said to him on the night she suggested the girls had pulled "the old switcheroo" came flooding back to him. He took a deep breath. "You girls don't want to tell me something, do you?"

"We only wanted to make you happy, Daddy." Caroline broke first, running to hug him around the waist.

"You wanted us to do good for Parents' Night so bad that you even said you'd break your rule." Hayley charged in to take up the rest of the story and to join her sister in the death grip of a hug.

"I did the square dance for Caroline and she did the mobile and the collage for Hayley and me." Juliette came flying, arms wide to complete the circle.

Only, for the first time since Marie had died, the circle did not seem complete to Sam.

Sam looked down on those three little redheads and realized there was something—someone—missing.

"How did you know, Daddy?" Hayley tipped her head back to look up and ask.

"I didn't know. Miss Bennett did and I guess you can figure out now how she knew." Sam turned his head to look Polly's way. "I just now put the pieces together when I saw two out of three girls dressed in pink. Makes it easier to trade places last-minute, huh?"

Caroline and Juliette bowed their heads, their way of 'fessing up to the plan.

"I think I had a clue when I saw that Juliette had managed to make a collage and still have a full bottle of pink glitter and that Hayley had a complete mobile hanging in her classroom and a half-finished one hanging above her desk at home."

He looked down at his daughters and his chest ached. What had he done? He had pushed his girls so hard to learn his way of coping that he'd forgotten to share with them things like waiting on the Lord, accepting God's will and trusting that there is a time for every purpose under heaven.

That had to change. He had to slow things down and…

He lifted his eyes to meet Polly's. "I don't suppose you want in on this, do you?"

"Sam, I'm a twin and a teacher, but that hardly qualifies me to talk to your kids about the moral implications of trading places to fool people."

Sam shook his head slowly and extended his hand,

making a space within the circle of his arms. "I meant do you want in on this group hug?"

Polly hesitated for a moment. She looked to her sister, who actually lowered her cell phone—she'd been on nonstop talking to her staff in Atlanta—for a moment. Esther nodded to urge Polly to hurry up.

Polly did just that, running with her own arms wide to embrace the man and the family she had waited so long to find.

Sam pressed his cheek to her soft but wild hair and drew her close. The girls entwined them both in a tangle of small arms, red hair and a million joyous giggles. In that moment Sam knew that his time for grieving had come to an end.

He laughed softly, then tipped his head back and looked at the sky. He groaned. "I suppose I looked like a real fool to you, Polly. Barreling through life like that, not even taking the time to see what the girls had gotten up to."

"No." She stepped back and took a minute to look at Hayley, then Juliette, then Caroline. "You look like a father who wants what's best for his daughters, but couldn't quite figure out what that was on his own."

"Maybe the problem is that I shouldn't be on my own?" He took her hand and guided her free of the cluster of kids, grinning.

"Don't you have a rule about that?" She smiled back at him.

"Hey, I make the rules." He got her far enough away that he could give her a spin and put them face-to-face again. "So if I finally get smart enough to change the rules, then wouldn't you say—"

"Sam?" She pressed two fingers to his lips.

"What?" he asked when she lowered her hand from his mouth.

"Stop while you're ahead and just kiss me," she murmured.

"I can do that." And he did. He pulled her deep into his embrace and kissed her.

The girls squealed with delight.

The crowd cheered.

The fire-engine siren wailed.

And out of nowhere a little golden-brown dog with floppy ears, short legs and a long, low body came bounding toward them.

"Donut!" The triplets ran for him.

The dog began to jump and bark and wag his tail and loll his tongue as if he wasn't sure which kid to start licking hello first.

Polly didn't know where to look. The dog. The girls. Essie. Sam.

Sam won out simply because she wanted to take her cue from him. She was so happy about having shared this moment with him, but she understood more than anyone Sam's fear of how much losing Donut again would hurt the girls. It was killing her not to run and hug the little guy.

"Hey, Donut."

"Oh, Donut."

"We love you, too, Donut."

"Grover! Grover! Come back here!" Ted Perry came pounding through the crowd, his face red and the chain leash in his fist banging against his legs. When he saw the girls hanging all over the wriggling pup, he stopped in his tracks.

"See?" Angela Bodine, the lady firefighter, came up behind him. "I told you! *That* is a kids' dog."

"He's *these* kids' dog!" Caroline announced, looking up at the pair who were now walking toward the opening in the crowd where the redheaded triplets and little golden-brown dog were all over each other.

"I know. He cries all the time and tries to push his way out the door whenever I open it." Ted sighed and shook his head. "Maybe I shoulda got a cat."

Angela's eyes brightened. "I love cats."

Ted jerked his head up. He looked at Sam, then Polly.

"I think I know where you could have your pick of a litter," Sam told him. "Don't suppose you'd want to make a trade?"

Ted opened his mouth as if he was going to say no, then he caught Angela practically bouncing out of her boots.

Ted grinned, swung his gaze around to meet Sam's and stuck his hand out to give Sam the leash and shake his hand. "You got a deal, man."

"That's *old* man, if you don't mind." Max slapped Sam hard on the back.

"He didn't look so old when he was kissing the schoolteacher a minute ago," Angela observed, then added, "You said something about kittens?"

"In the barn," Max directed her absently, then looked up, saw her and offered her his arm. "I'd be happy to show you."

Ted stepped in between the charmer in sandals and

a barbecue apron, and the lady firefighter. "I think we can find it on our own."

Max threw up his hands. "Is every single lady in this town already attached to someone else?"

"Not *every* one." Polly dipped her head toward Essie coming across the open space. She could see by the box in her sister's hand that Esther had gone to the car to retrieve the hat Polly had picked out online long before she ever really believed she'd be standing here with Sam's arm around her.

"Well, well, well." Max rubbed his palms together. "Hello, pretty lady. Can I help you with that?"

"I don't need help with this. Just hand it to my sister." She pushed the box into his chest. "Then follow me back over to that grill area. Because you are in need of some serious help if you plan to cook actual food, mister."

"I like her," Max said as he handed Polly the box. "Can I keep her?"

Sam and Polly laughed and watched Max trying to corral Essie, who had already taken charge of the situation.

"Can we take Donut into the house and show him his new home, Daddy?" Caroline asked before she turned to Polly and added, "That is, if you aren't going to take him home with you, Miss Bennett."

Polly went all gooey at Caroline's thoughtfulness. "Angela was right, sweetie. Donut will be happiest with kids around. I'd love for him to stay with you, as long as I can visit sometimes."

"Anytime!" Hayley yelled to speak for the triplets and her whole family.

The other girls leaped up. They all called for Donut and began to run through the crowd toward the house.

"I really am glad Donut is going to have a home with you and the girls." Polly hugged the hatbox close, not exactly sure what to do next.

He'd said he was ready to change his rules and did just that by letting the girls have Donut. But what did that mean for her?

The fire-engine siren sounded again. This time followed by a blare of microphone feedback, a fumble broadcast over a loudspeaker and then Gina's voice. "I'd like to welcome you all to the Goodacre Organic Farm's Annual Pumpkin Jump."

She listed all the events, booths and performances as people gathered in a semicircle around her, listening. "And at last the time has come to open the main event of the day, the thing that this fest is named for— the big pumpkin jump on the main lawn!"

A cheer went up from the group. The girls, after leaving Donut safely in the house, rejoined Polly and Sam standing to the side. Max and Essie had wandered over from his burger fry booth, leaving a volunteer in charge.

"Are you going to jump this year, Daddy?" Hayley prodded.

"I, um, don't you girls think that's kind of embarrassing behavior for the local pharmacist?" Sam bent down to ask them eye to eye.

"You're asking me?" Caroline stuck her thumb in her chest. "I'm going to have to do that square dance!"

Sam gave the three of them a stern look. "Yes, you

are. And we'll talk about the punishment for pulling the old switcheroo later."

"Yes, Daddy." They looked properly chastised for maybe three whole seconds before their faces brightened and they asked again, "Are you going to jump, Daddy?"

He turned to Polly. "Actually, I'd love to jump…if Polly is willing to take the leap with me."

Polly's heart raced. "You mean, into the leaves, right?"

"I was thinking more of…into the future." He took her free hand in his, then reached for the hatbox. "Can I set this aside?"

"Actually, you can set it on your head, if you want. That's not being flip, it's just…well, look inside the box." She bit her lower lip.

The girls gathered around.

He lifted off the lid, looked inside and grinned. He pulled out the vintage-style hat and put it on his head. The perfect fit.

"You look handsome, Daddy," Caroline said.

Polly couldn't have agreed more. There with the autumn leaves tumbling around them, the sights and sounds of Sam's family's home in full-on local celebration, he looked perfect.

"I like it!" Hayley cried.

"I like it a whole lot better than that awful cowboy hat." Juliette crinkled up her nose.

"Me, too." Sam laughed as he tugged the hat to put it at an angle over one eye. "I never did like that cowboy hat. How's that?"

"It's you! I got it for you to replace the… Wait!"

What Sam had said just sank in. All these weeks she had worried and mulled over the meaning of what she had done to that hat and how Sam had reacted to it. "You never liked that cowboy hat?"

"You did me a favor by not stopping Donut from grabbing it. It was the start of all this." He tossed the hatbox aside and opened his arms wide. "Marie gave it to me as a gentle reminder to not become like the rancher dad in her *No, No, Donut* story."

"You mean the man who chased the little dog away and thought the dog could never learn?" Polly laughed.

"The man who had forgotten the power of God's grace and the healing power of faith and forgiveness." He came toward her, his arms still open.

"I don't think that sounds like you at all, Sam." She came into his arms again. "Maybe at one time. But now?"

"Now is what matters." He closed his arms around her. "The past is out of our control and the future is in God's hands. So what do you say, Polly Bennett? You going to take the leap? Are you going to marry me?"

"Yes," she murmured as he pulled her close and kissed her in the way she had longed to be kissed ever since she saw him.

Polly wrapped her arms around him and kissed him right back. Kissed him with all the joy and confidence she had been missing for so long.

For the first time since this whole adventure began, Polly believed she had found everything she had been searching for since her own family began to unravel all those years ago. She had found the insight to forgive her parents their shortcomings. To reevaluate her relationship with her twin sister and to follow her own dreams to make herself feel productive and fulfilled. And she had found Sam.

"Marry?" Essie's voice drew Polly back to the present. "After only knowing each other a couple of months? Isn't that rushing things?"

Polly pulled away and looked up at Sam sheepishly. "Small towns, huh? People who are always there for you are also always there whether you want them to be or not."

"Do you mind?" he asked.

"I love it," she whispered. "And I love you, Sam Goodacre."

"I love you, too, Polly. Now, hold on to your hat… or rather, *my* hat." He thrust it out in the direction of Essie and Max.

They both reached for it and their hands touched. Suddenly neither of them seemed to have anything more to say.

Sam took Polly by the hand. "Let's do this!"

They made the run without reservations and leaped without fear. Seconds after they hit the leaf pile and came up in a shower of red and yellow and orange and pale green leaves, three little red-haired girls joined them. Polly's heart was fuller than she'd ever thought a human heart could be, and as she threw her arms around her future husband and daughters, she sent up a prayer of thanks.

* * * * *

Dear Reader,

My children have said for years that I should write a children's book and title it *No, No, Donut!* just like the story in this book. They got the idea because it's such a frequent phrase heard around our house about one of our dogs, of course named Donut. Of our own triple threat, Donut is the clown who always seems to get into mischief but is so full of love that just to look at him makes your heart sigh. He has taught us much about the nature of love, of giving of oneself fully and of knowing when to be humble in asking forgiveness. Isn't it funny how a small mixed-breed mutt can be the source of such spiritual lessons?

That's why I was so pleased to do a story involving a little lost dog, a family who needed healing and a heroine just trying to find out who she is and where she belongs. It has been great fun to create the Goodacre family and the character of Polly Bennett and to mix in a little of my own personal life with Donut, the dog who just wanted to be loved, as we all do.

Annie Jones

Questions for Discussion

1. Have you ever considered a move to start over as Polly Bennett did?

2. Sam Goodacre made some simple rule he thought would protect his daughters. Do you think it's realistic that a single father would do that? Why or why not?

3. Do you think identical twins or multiples have a special bond that is different than the bond between other siblings?

4. Ecclesiastes teaches to everything there is a season. The characters are moving from one season of their lives to the next. Do you see how this has applied to your life?

5. The hero lives on his family's farm. Have you ever lived on a farm? Would you want to? Why or why not?

6. The heroine thinks life has become too rushed. Would you agree?

7. The heroine also feels that not all children should be pushed, and they should be left to learn at their own pace. Do you agree or not?

8. The hero is attracted to the heroine early, but

avoids a relationship to spare his children's feelings. Do you think this is a wise choice?

9. One thing the hero has to learn is to wait on the Lord. Do you find this a difficult thing to do in life?

10. The characters enjoy small-town life despite some of the drawbacks. Do you think you would (or do you) enjoy life in a small town? Why or why not?

11. There is a small substory about being a cat person or a dog person—which are you?

12. The triplets exchange places and fool some people in the school. Do you think this is realistic or that someone's individuality always comes through?

13. The heroine selects for the hero a hat that symbolizes the new kind of relationship they have. Have you ever given someone a symbolic accessory? What was it?

14. The story refers to a special bedtime story that helps the children learn a lesson. Do you have a favorite bedtime story, either that you were told or that you told your children?

15. The story concludes with the hero and heroine jumping into a pile of leaves. Do you have a story about having done that and how it made you feel?

INSPIRATIONAL

Love Inspired®

COMING NEXT MONTH
AVAILABLE MARCH 27, 2012

HER LONE STAR COWBOY
Mule Hollow Homecoming
Debra Clopton

A LOVE REKINDLED
A Town Called Hope
Margaret Daley

SWEETHEART REUNION
Lenora Worth

REDEMPTION RANCH
Leann Harris

HER FAMILY WISH
Betsy St. Amant

LOVE OF A LIFETIME
Carol Voss

REQUEST YOUR FREE BOOKS!

2 FREE INSPIRATIONAL NOVELS
PLUS 2
FREE
MYSTERY GIFTS

YES! Please send me 2 FREE Love Inspired® novels and my 2 FREE mystery gifts (gifts are worth about $10). After receiving them, if I don't wish to receive any more books, I can return the shipping statement marked "cancel." If I don't cancel, I will receive 6 brand-new novels every month and be billed just $4.49 per book in the U.S. or $4.99 per book in Canada. That's a saving of at least 22% off the cover price. It's quite a bargain! Shipping and handling is just 50¢ per book in the U.S. and 75¢ per book in Canada.* I understand that accepting the 2 free books and gifts places me under no obligation to buy anything. I can always return a shipment and cancel at any time. Even if I never buy another book, the two free books and gifts are mine to keep forever.

105/305 IDN FEGR

Name _____ (PLEASE PRINT)

Address _____ Apt. #

City _____ State/Prov. _____ Zip/Postal Code

Signature (if under 18, a parent or guardian must sign)

Mail to the **Reader Service**:
IN U.S.A.: P.O. Box 1867, Buffalo, NY 14240-1867
IN CANADA: P.O. Box 609, Fort Erie, Ontario L2A 5X3

Not valid for current subscribers to Love Inspired books.

**Are you a subscriber to Love Inspired books
and want to receive the larger-print edition?
Call 1-800-873-8635 or visit www.ReaderService.com.**

* Terms and prices subject to change without notice. Prices do not include applicable taxes. Sales tax applicable in N.Y. Canadian residents will be charged applicable taxes. Offer not valid in Quebec. This offer is limited to one order per household. All orders subject to credit approval. Credit or debit balances in a customer's account(s) may be offset by any other outstanding balance owed by or to the customer. Please allow 4 to 6 weeks for delivery. Offer available while quantities last.

Your Privacy—The Reader Service is committed to protecting your privacy. Our Privacy Policy is available online at www.ReaderService.com or upon request from the Reader Service.

We make a portion of our mailing list available to reputable third parties that offer products we believe may interest you. If you prefer that we not exchange your name with third parties, or if you wish to clarify or modify your communication preferences, please visit us at www.ReaderService.com/consumerschoice or write to us at Reader Service Preference Service, P.O. Box 9062, Buffalo, NY 14269. Include your complete name and address.

LIREG11B

celebrating **15** YEARS **Love Inspired**

Kim Walters needs Zane Davidson's help. After a devastating hurricane, Kim's family is struggling to rebuild their home, and Zane is a successful contractor. But it's been fifteen years since they were high school sweethearts and their past problems aren't about to magically melt away. Can Kim and Zane find the faith to believe that some things work better the second time around?

A Love Rekindled
by Margaret Daley

Available April wherever books are sold.

www.LoveInspiredBooks.com

For a sneak peek of Shirlee McCoy's heart-stopping inspirational romantic suspense
UNDERCOVER BODYGUARD, read on!

"It's okay," Ryder said, pulling Shelby into his arms.

But it wasn't okay, and they both knew it.

A woman was dead, and there was nothing either of them could do to change it.

"How can it be when Maureen is dead?" Shelby asked, looking up into his face as if he might have some way to fix things. He didn't, and he'd stopped believing in his own power and invincibility long ago.

"It will be. Eventually. Come on. You need to get the bump on your head looked at."

"I don't have time for that. I have to get back to the bakery. It's Friday. The busiest day of the week." Her teeth chattered on the last word, her body trembling. He draped his coat around her shoulders.

"Better?" he asked, and she nodded.

"I can't seem to stop shaking. I mean, one minute, I'm preparing to deliver pastries to my friend and the next she's gone. I just can't believe…." Her voice trailed off, her eyes widening as she caught sight of his gun holster.

"You've got a gun."

"Yes."

"Are you a police officer?"

"Security contractor."

"You're a bodyguard?"

"I'm a security contractor. I secure people and things."

"A bodyguard," she repeated, and he didn't argue.

Two fire trucks and an ambulance lined the curb in front of the house, and firefighters had already hooked a hose to the hydrant. Water streamed over the flames but did little to douse the fire.

Suddenly, an EMT ran toward them. "Is she okay?"

"She was knocked unconscious by the force of the explosion. She has a bad gash on her head."

"Let me take a look." The EMT edged him out of the way, and Ryder knew it was time to go talk to the fire marshal and the police officers who'd just arrived, and let the EMT take Shelby to the hospital.

But she grabbed his hand before he moved away, her grip surprisingly strong. "Are you leaving?"

"Do you want me to, Shelby Ann?" he asked.

"You can leave."

"I know that I can, but do you *want* me to?"

"I...haven't decided, yet."

Pick up UNDERCOVER BODYGUARD for the rest of Shelby and Ryder's exciting, suspenseful love story, available in April 2012, only from Love Inspired® Books Love Inspired® Suspense.